THE BIG BOOK OF AMAZING ANIMALS

Text by
Anton Ericson, Celia Brand, Donald Olson, Esther Reisberg,
Jane P. Resnick, John Grassy, Katharine Smith, Kerry Acker,
Mary Kay Carson, Rebecca L. Grambo, Robert Matero

Photo Credits
Bigstock, Dreamstime, Fotolia, iStockphoto, Shutterstock

Kidsbooks®

Visit us at www.kidsbooks.com

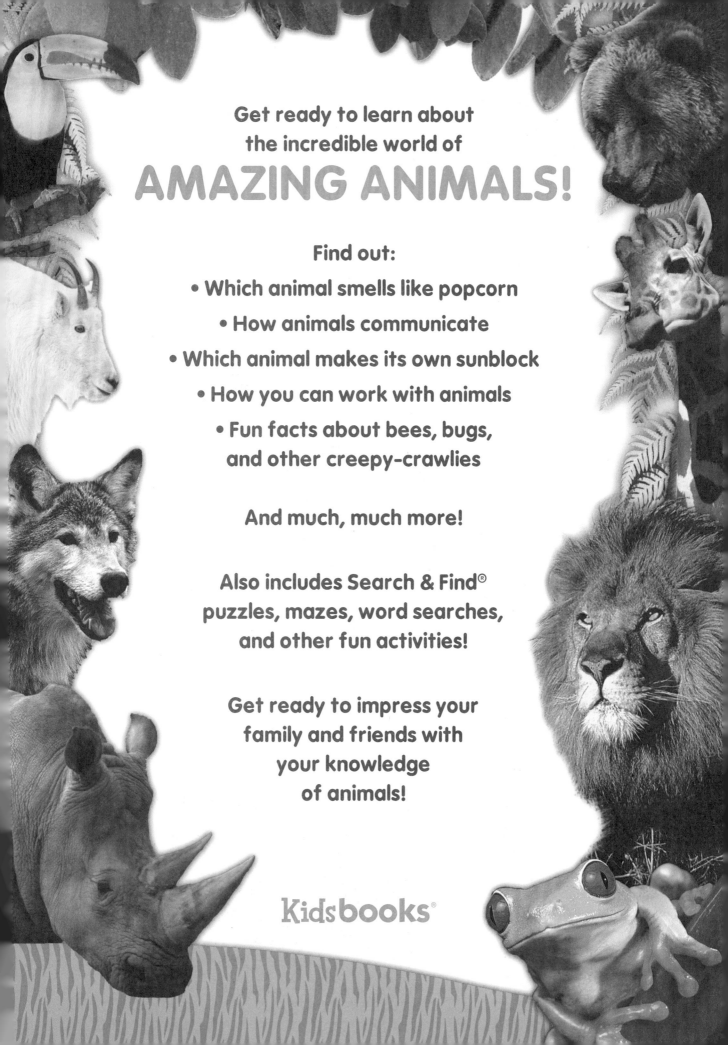

Get ready to learn about
the incredible world of

AMAZING ANIMALS!

Find out:

- Which animal smells like popcorn

- How animals communicate

- Which animal makes its own sunblock

- How you can work with animals

- Fun facts about bees, bugs,
and other creepy-crawlies

And much, much more!

Also includes Search & Find®
puzzles, mazes, word searches,
and other fun activities!

Get ready to impress your
family and friends with
your knowledge
of animals!

Kidsbooks®

Animal Groups

Animals are divided into two large groups: vertebrates, animals with a spine or backbone, and invertebrates, animals without a spine.

Mammals, birds, fish, reptiles, and amphibians are all vertebrates.

Mammal Members

Mammals include dolphins, bats, foxes, and lions. You're a mammal, too!

Mammals Are...

All mammals have hair and are warm-blooded, breathe air, and nurse their young.

INSECTS, SPIDERS, JELLYFISH, WORMS, AND CORAL ARE ALL INVERTEBRATES.

Today's Count

About 4,000 species of mammals exist today. The squirrel and its rodent relatives make up the largest mammal group—in number of species and number of individual animals.

Reptiles are cold-blooded and have very dry, scaly skin.

Out of Water

Amphibians are also cold-blooded and are born in the water. When they grow up, they can live on land.

Classifying Animals

Classification is the system scientists use to name and organize all organisms, or living things, into groups.

There are seven levels, or groups, of classification, and each group gets smaller and smaller from the first to the last. As you go down the line through each level, you'll notice that the smaller the group, the fewer animals it includes and the more those animals have in common.

The groups are called:

kingdom
phylum
class
order
family
genus
species

A fun way to remember the order is to make up sentences using the first letter of each level. Here are a few examples:

Kings Prefer Clothes Of Fine Gold Silk

Kids Play Catch Or Fun Games Sunday

Keep Particular Creatures Organized For Good Scientists

The animal kingdom is one of five major kingdoms. The other four are plants, bacteria, fungi, and protists (single-celled creatures like algae).

What do humans have in common with the golden lion tamarin?

Let's take a look at how each species is classified to find out!

Humans (*Homo sapiens*)	Golden Lion Tamarin (*Leontopithecus rosalia*)
Kingdom = Animal	Kingdom = Animal
Phylum = Chordata (vertebrate)	Phylum = Chordata
Class = Mammalia (mammal)	Class = Mammalia
Order = Primates	Order = Primates
Family = Hominidae	Family = Callitrichidae
Genus = *Homo*	Genus = *Leontopithecus*
Species = *sapiens*	Species = *L. rosalia*

Working with Animals

Doctors for animals are called VETERINARIANS, or VETS. Vets take care of all kinds of animals, from pets and farm animals to exotic and wild animals. Some vets don't work directly with animals. Teaching or research vets study animal health to help protect animals from illness in the future.

MARINE BIOLOGISTS study creatures that live in the ocean. They work in laboratories, on boats, or in submarines.

A ZOOLOGIST studies the behavior and characteristics of animals, both living and extinct, often observing animals in their natural habitats and writing reports about them.

ANIMAL CONTROL OFFICERS inspect kennels, shelters, pet shops, and other places where animals live in order to make sure they are safe and healthy environments. They also rescue trapped or injured animals from unhealthy homes and work with police and fire departments to save animals.

A WILDLIFE REHABILITATOR helps heal sick or injured wild animals. Once an animal is healthy enough to survive on its own, it is released back into the wild. Otherwise the rehabilitated, or healed, animal is taken to a wildlife refuge.

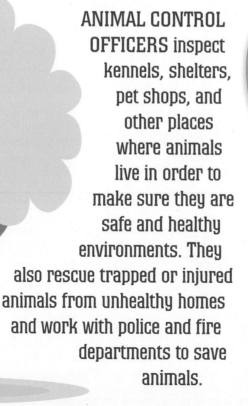

An ANIMAL TRAINER teaches animals to do certain jobs. For example, a trainer may teach dogs how to do everyday tasks so they can become service dogs. Trainers also help humans teach their pets obedience.

Animals can be therapists! Animals like dogs are often brought into hospitals and nursing homes to cheer people up and to help with things like physical therapy!

A PET GROOMER makes sure your pets look good! Groomers bathe animals, cut their fur and nails, and clean their teeth.

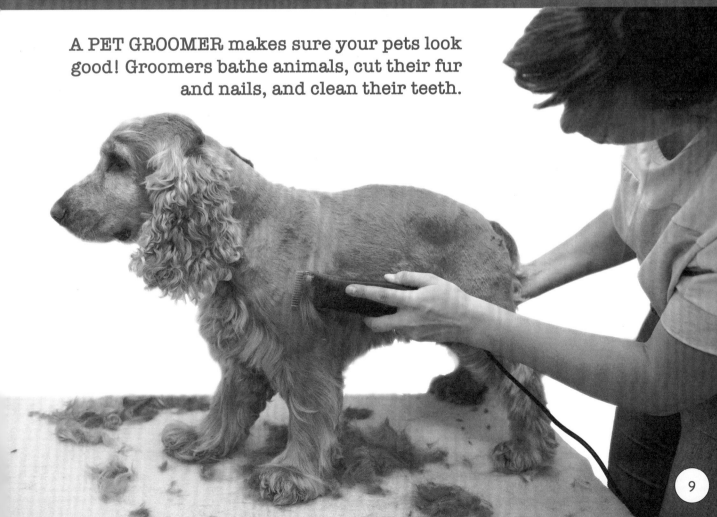

Word Scramble

Amazing Animal Jobs

Unscramble the letters to spell the names of animal jobs.
Which job sounds the most exciting to you?
Write it down in the space at the bottom of the page!

LSTOGOIOZ

_ _ _ _ _ _ _ _ _

MANALI RENTIAR

_ _ _ _ _ _ _ _ _ _ _ _

EPT ROERGOM

_ _ _ _ _ _ _ _ _

LAMINA TORLCON RECFOIF

_ _ _ _ _ _ _ _ _ _ _ _ _ _ _ _ _ _ _ _

NAVEINATIRER

_ _ _ _ _ _ _ _ _ _ _ _

NALIMA SITRATHPE

_ _ _ _ _ _ _ _ _ _ _ _ _ _

Amphibians

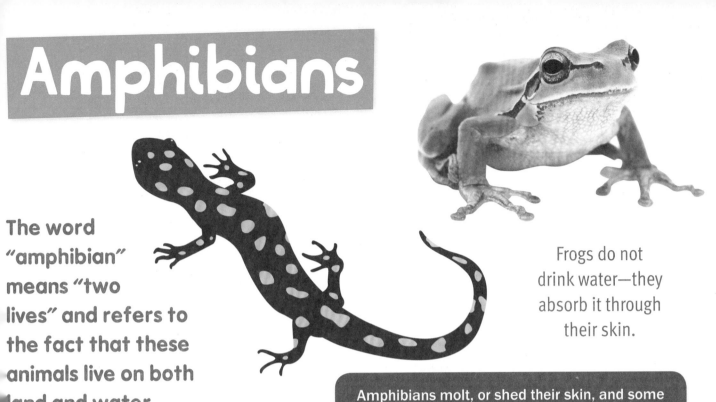

The word "amphibian" means "two lives" and refers to the fact that these animals live on both land and water.

Frogs do not drink water—they absorb it through their skin.

Amphibians molt, or shed their skin, and some even eat the skin afterward to gain nutrients.

Fun Facts
about the
Wood Frog

The wood frog may seem like an ordinary frog, but it can do something extraordinary: It can freeze itself on purpose! In cold places like Alaska, the wood frog hides underground or under rocks or leaves and becomes completely frozen. In the spring, the frog thaws and begins moving around again.

The wood frog's call is a quacking sound!

Wood frogs can jump farther than most other frogs.

Reptiles

FUNKY FrILLS

The Australian frilled lizard spends most of its life in trees. If cornered on the ground, however, it rears on its back legs, extends the enormous frill around its head, opens its mouth wide, and hisses.

Third Eye

One of the tuatara's most interesting features is the third "eye" located on the top of its brain. It is sensitive to light but cannot see images like a true eye. It also is covered with skin, which gets darker over time.

Rainbow Scales
Chameleons change colors to display a reaction or emotion.

Snap to It!

Instead of teeth, turtles have beak-like jaws with sharp edges, which chop plants and small animals into bite-sized pieces. The prehistoric-looking alligator snapping turtle uses its strong, sharp beak to deliver a vicious bite.

SHELL SHOCK

A TURTLE'S SHELL IS PART OF ITS SKELETON. THE CURVED UPPER PART, CALLED THE CARAPACE, IS MADE OF THE TURTLE'S RIBS AND BACKBONE. THE FLATTER LOWER PART, CALLED THE PLASTRON, IS MADE OF SPECIAL RIBS FOUND ON THE TURTLE'S BELLY.

Carapace

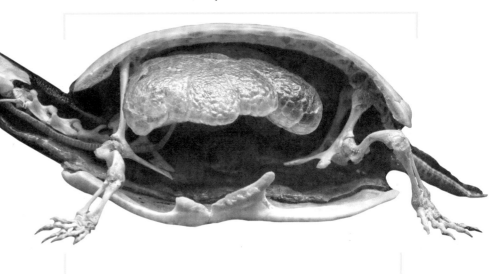

Plastron

Worm or Lizard?

Lizards without legs look a lot like small snakes—or huge worms. The slowworm spends most of its time burrowing underground, where it hunts for insects and worms.

SHEDDING SKIN

Reptiles' thick, scaly skin prevents their bodies from drying out. Snakes and some lizards shed skin as they grow. Lizard skin falls off in flakes, but snakes shed their entire skin at one time.

Canine Cousins

Family Matters

Dogs are descended from wolves, which are part of the same family as coyotes, jackals, and foxes. In the wild, these canids live and hunt in small groups and show powerful loyalty to their leader.

PALS THAT HOWL

To people, the howl of the wolf is the sound of the wild. To wolves, it may be a party. Wolves most often howl as a pack—to encourage their closeness, to celebrate a successful hunt, to find separated members, and to tell other packs to keep back. On a calm night, howling can broadcast 120 square miles.

BUILT JUST RIGHT

Coyotes have the tools to be excellent hunters: With their powerful legs, they can leap up to 14 feet. Keen eyesight and sharp hearing help detect the faintest stirrings of prey, and a strong sense of smell picks up human scent so coyotes can run to safety.

TOY STORY

AT THE SMALL END OF THE SCALE ARE THE TOY DOGS, BRED ORIGINALLY AS HOUSE (OR CASTLE) PETS FOR KINGS, QUEENS, AND NOBLES. THE IDEA WAS TO PRODUCE DOGS THAT COULD EASILY BE CARRIED FROM PLACE TO PLACE AND CRADLED ON LAPS.

Comrades in Arms

In ancient Britain, mastiffs fought side by side with their masters against Julius Caesar's Roman warriors. Centuries later, when the English knight Sir Piers Legh was wounded at the Battle of Agincourt, his loyal mastiff defended him for hours until help arrived.

Fierce Felines

The One and Only

Cheetahs are some of the most unique wild cats: Their claws do not fully retract; they cannot roar; and they are unable to climb trees. Cheetahs hunt primarily during the day to avoid running into other predators, like lions, that might steal their prey. They do have large lungs, a strong heart, and a slender, well-muscled body, built for speed.

Treetop Dining

A leopard does not invite guests to dinner. In fact, this expert climber often drags its kill up a tree to keep it safe. A leopard can climb a tree with a carcass weighing more than 50 pounds clamped in its jaws. The cat stows the victim over a branch, then takes a good rest knowing that its next meal is close by.

Water Cats

Jaguars are one of the few wild cat species that don't avoid water. They are great swimmers and use rivers and streams to play, hunt, and fish. These felines will even swim across the Panama Canal in order to breed!

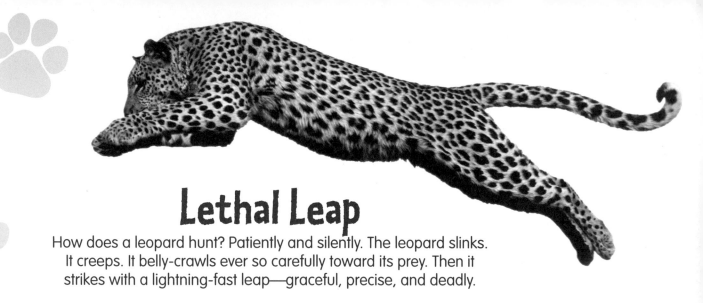

Lethal Leap

How does a leopard hunt? Patiently and silently. The leopard slinks. It creeps. It belly-crawls ever so carefully toward its prey. Then it strikes with a lightning-fast leap—graceful, precise, and deadly.

A Matter of Pride

Lions are the only cats that live in groups, called prides. Prides are usually made up of 15 or more individuals, but prides can have as few as three or as many as 40 cats. They all live together in a distinct territory, which can extend as far as 10 miles in any direction. The lionesses, which are usually related, inherit the home range, so they must be especially proud of their pride.

Old Souls

Tigers have been roaming the planet for a very long time–fossil remains of an extinct tiger species were found in China and believed to be over 2 million years old. These cats are silent hunters, but they know how to make themselves heard: A tiger's roar can be heard up to 2 miles away!

Food Chain
Carnivores

Carnivores are animals that eat other animals. Some examples of carnivores are snakes, spiders, and lions.

A food chain is a sequence that shows how living things get their food, and how energy and nutrients are passed from creature to creature.

Top of the Chain

If a carnivore doesn't have any animals that hunt it, it is called an apex predator. Examples of apex predators are tigers and crocodiles.

Carnivores are extremely good hunters and often have sharp teeth and claws to help them catch their prey

Leafy Predators

Plants can be carnivores, too! There are more than 600 species of carnivorous plants that trap and eat insects, small frogs, and small mammals.

THE SMALLEST CARNIVORE ON EARTH IS THE LEAST WEASEL.

Carnivores that mainly eat fish are called piscivores, like these giant otters.

PREMADE MEALS

Some carnivores aren't hunters and are called scavengers. They eat dead animals, called carrion, that have died or been killed by other animals.

Big Danger

Tusk Danger

Both male and female African elephants grow tusks. An elephant uses its tusks to dig for food and water and to scrape bark from trees. Elephants also use tusks for self defense, and males use them to fight over mates.

The Greatest

The great white shark is one of the largest, most deadly predators. Credited with more attacks on humans than any other shark, the average great white grows to about 15 feet long and can weigh up to 3,000 pounds. Twenty-foot great whites have also been reported!

Wide Mouth

The hippopotamus has sharp tusks that can grow to 28 inches long. The hippo uses them to fight and to threaten attackers, opening its mouth wide to reveal its tusks. If that is not enough to scare the challenger away, a fight follows—sometimes to the death.

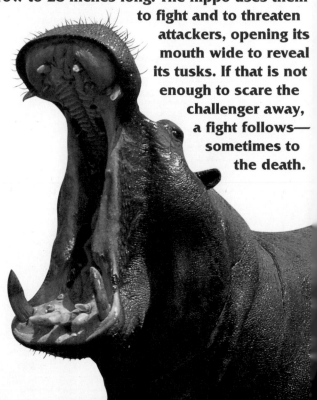

Powerful Jaws

With one snap, an alligator's jaws are powerful enough to crack a turtle shell. However, the muscles used to open its mouth are so weak that, once shut, the jaws can easily be held together. All crocodilians are flesh eaters and feed on any animals they can catch—from birds and fish to zebras or antelopes.

THE KING AND QUEEN OF BEASTS

The lion is known as the King of Beasts for good reason: A male lion can weigh as much as 500 pounds, and the female is no less royal at up to 300. The male protects the pride and defends the females against intruders, while the females do most of the hunting.

GIANT LIZARD

Weighing up to 300 pounds or more, the fierce Komodo dragon is the heaviest living lizard on Earth. This predator will eat nearly anything it can find, dead or alive, including deer and wild boar, and, occasionally, humans!

Animal Habitats
African Savanna

The different environments in which animals live are called habitats.

Meow?

Although hyenas appear similar to dogs, especially the African wild dog, they are actually more closely related to cats. They find food by hunting prey and scavenging the remains of dead animals.

Wildebeests and zebras are grazers, which means they feed on grass.

Who Gnu?

The wildebeest is also known as a gnu. It's a member of the antelope family, though it more closely resembles a cow!

Though they are not a type of horse, zebras share many similarities with horses: they both have hard hooves, live and graze in herds, and have similar body shapes.

THE AFRICAN SAVANNA IS A HABITAT MADE UP OF OPEN, TROPICAL GRASSLANDS. THE SAVANNA IS HOT AND DRY DURING HALF OF THE YEAR, WHEN WILDFIRES SWEEP ACROSS THE LAND. THERE IS ALSO A RAINY SEASON, WHICH HELPS TALL GRASSES GROW.

Number One Runner

The cheetah is the fastest land animal on Earth. Running at high speeds uses a lot of energy, so the cheetah can only sprint short distances. This amazing, deadly sprint is the cheetah's most important weapon—it runs for its supper and runs for its life.

Pack Animals

Wildebeests move through the African savanna in huge herds of up to 100,000 animals.

The Arctic

Atlantic Puffin

This bird may look like a penguin, but it's a puffin! The puffin has a colorful beak that fades in the winter and brightens in the spring. Apart from returning to land for breeding season, puffins spend most of their time swimming or floating on the water.

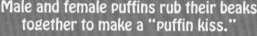
Male and female puffins rub their beaks together to make a "puffin kiss."

Harp Seal

Harp seals can easily dive down 600 feet. That is like diving off a tall city building!

Baby harp seals are born with white fur to help camouflage them in the snow. As they get older, their fur turns a grayish color.

The Arctic is at the northernmost point on Earth and includes the North Pole. This region contains the Arctic Ocean, with floating ice at the center, and the northern tips of many countries.

Polar Bear

Polar bears have pads of rough skin on the bottom of their feet that help them grip the ice and snow.

MOOSE

Unlike their deer cousins, moose travel alone, not in herds.

Arctic Fox

Arctic foxes have fur that changes color to help them blend with their surroundings in different seasons: white in winter, tan or brown in summer.

Furry Farm Friends

Moo! Who's that Cow?

It's one of the most popular dairy cows there is! This black-and-white cow is called Holstein-Friesian. These types of cows are popular with farmers because they produce a lot of milk.

All cows are female, and milk comes from their udders. Can you think of other animals that produce milk?

A baby cow is called a calf.

THE FOLKS

An adult female horse is called a mare, and an adult male horse is called a stallion. Mares and stallions mate during the spring—a time when food is more plentiful in the wild.

Foaling Around

A female foal, or young horse, is called a filly; a male foal is called a colt. As they grow, colts and fillies love to play. Running together teaches foals about survival behavior.

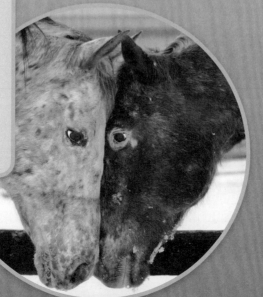

Nap Time

A foal, like all babies, needs plenty of rest and frequently takes naps. At the first sign of danger, however, a foal quickly gets to its feet and runs to its mother's side.

Pony Tales

Ponies are technically horses, but they are much smaller. Ponies usually grow no higher than 58 inches—yet they are sturdier on their feet than the horse.

MINIATURE HORSES

Miniature horses are not ponies. This breed of horse averages 30 inches in height to the shoulder. Known to be good-tempered and friendly, miniature horses have been bred as pets and service animals.

Night Life

Creatures that are active at night and sleep during the day are called nocturnal animals.

Handy Mammal

Raccoons use their fingers to open doors, eat food, and pick up objects, similar to the way humans use their hands.

Flying lemurs are also known as colugos. Like bats and flying squirrels, these mammals are mostly nocturnal. Colugos have large flaps of skin that help them glide through the air.

Cleaning Up

Found throughout much of the Americas, the raccoon is known for ransacking garbage cans and scattering trash in residential communities. It also has a reputation for "washing" its food—exploring the object with its paws—even in the absence of water. The name "raccoon" comes from the Algonquian Native American word *arahkun*, meaning "he scratches with his hands."

The hedgehog has quite a diverse diet: It will eat worms, centipedes, mice, frogs, and even snakes. This mammal gets its name because it forages, or searches for food, by digging through hedges and other undergrowth.

Fun Facts about Bats

Bats make up one-fifth of the world's mammals.

Bats sleep hanging upside down.

Bats live together in colonies of 100 to 1,000 members.

All Talk

SMART TALKER

Apes are great communicators. One famous gorilla named Koko, who lives at The Gorilla Foundation, has even learned to use more than 500 words in American Sign Language. For her 25th birthday, Koko asked for a box of "scary" rubber snakes and lizards!

Wolf Talk

Wolves communicate their feelings through gestures and body movements.

HONEYBEES COMMUNICATE THROUGH DANCING.

In Good Voice

Coyotes are musical. Their voices have a high and low range. Their howling is very close to singing, with a variety of sounds—barks, huffs, yelps, woofs, and yaps. They recognize each other's voices. When one coyote begins howling, others within hearing distance join in. Mated coyotes keep in touch through howling when separated. They even have a greeting sound.

TUNE FOR TWO

All penguin pairs "sing" a duet as part of their display, and it's not just for entertainment. This helps them learn to recognize each other's voices. That's very important, because there are thousands of look-alikes in a rookery, or group of penguins on land.

TOUGH TALK

Cats have their own communication system: hissing, spitting, growling, and snarling. Purring, the perfect sound of contentment, is for pleasure.

Chatter

Although they are fairly quiet, bears do communicate with sound. They growl when threatened and hum when content. They even whine and cry when they're upset.

Poisonous Predators

VENOMOUS VIPERS

A viper keeps its extra-long fangs folded back against the roof of its mouth—until it's ready to strike. Vipers have wide heads in which they store their large venom glands. Gaboon vipers, found in tropical African forests, have the longest fangs of any snake—up to 2 inches!

Hooded Terror

The 18-foot king cobra is the longest poisonous snake in the world, with venom powerful enough to kill an elephant. When threatened, it spreads the loose skin on its neck into a "hood" several times wider than its body. Moving with its upper body raised off the ground, a hooded cobra is indeed a fearsome sight! Aggressive baby cobras, armed with fangs and venom, will strike while still emerging from their shells.

KOMODO CLAWS

The Komodo dragon's long, forked tongue flicks in and out of its mouth, sensing both taste and smell. This reptile's powerful claws can cause serious damage during a fight with other lizards. A hunting Komodo dragon bites its prey. If the bite does not kill right away, the infection from a Komodo dragon's drool will do so before long.

Fun Facts about Poison Arrow Frogs

The poison arrow frog, also called the poison dart frog, is a brightly colored, tiny amphibian that lives in the rain forests of Central and South America. No more than 1 inch long, this little frog's skin can be green, blue, red, yellow, or orange. Although beautiful, its skin is also this frog's best means of defense.

Mucus Defense

The skin of a poison arrow frog is covered in mucus. This helps the frog stay moist when it's away from water, and it helps tadpoles stay attached to the mother. However, the mucus also contains one of the most powerful poisons in the world! This poison has to be strong, because many of the poison arrow frog's predators, such as snakes and spiders, are not harmed by weaker poisons.

Poison Attack

If a predator licks a poison arrow frog, it will get very sick, very quickly, and will never attack again. The poison enters the predator's bloodstream and affects nerves and muscles. Sometimes, just one lick can be fatal!

LIGHT EYES

Unlike many other frog species, poison arrow frogs are more active during the day and sleep at night.

Frog Medicine

Long used by Ecuadorian Choco Indians as a weapon, the venom from the poison arrow frog can help as well as hurt. One compound in the venom acts as a painkiller that is 200 times better at fighting pain than is morphine, a drug used in hospitals.

Hunting Skills

Native people in South America apply the poison that comes from the skin of these frogs to darts and arrowheads for hunting small animals.

Penguin Pals

Will the real penguin please stand up? There are 17 species of penguins, and no two are exactly alike!

Voices Carry

Penguins communicate by "calling"—a cross between trumpets blaring and donkeys braying. Each species has its own call. Each penguin has its own sound, and individuals locate one another by voice.

The emperor penguin is the largest of the penguin species, measuring 3½ feet tall and weighing over 60 pounds. That's a lot of bird!

PENGUIN PAIRS

Most penguins stick to the same partner. One theory for this behavior is that most return to their old territory and meet up automatically, but some scientists believe that penguins recognize each other by voice and sight, even after a year.

Feathered Friends

The macaroni penguin is named for its crest of orange and yellow feathers, which resembles a popular hairstyle for young men in England during the late 1700s and early 1800s.

Penguin Maze
Home Sweet Home

Ever get lost? Imagine looking for your parents among thousands of others! Luckily, in the penguin world, chicks and parents recognize each other's calls and always find one another. A chick calls out even as it breaks out of its egg so the parent will get to know its voice.

This baby penguin wandered away from the rookery and got lost! Follow the maze to help the baby penguin find his mom.

START

FINISH

Answers on page 222

In the Trees

Ape or Monkey?

Besides their large size, apes are different from monkeys in other ways. They don't have a tail, and they "knuckle-walk" on their front hands. Monkeys scamper about on the flats of their palms.

BLUSHER

The uakari (wah-CAR-ee) has a red face and bald head. It's an amazingly expressive monkey: When really angry or excited, its face turns even brighter. If it feels threatened, it shakes the branches and makes a noise that sounds like laughter.

smart SKILLS

The capuchin monkey is a highly intelligent monkey living in the Amazon rain forest. It uses objects in its environment as basic tools, cracking open nuts with stones or gathering bunches of leaves into a sponge to soak up fruit juice.

Chimp Pals

Friendships among chimpanzees are very strong and can last for many years, even if one chimp should take up with another group. When two chimp friends meet after a period of separation, they hug, kiss, and pat each other on the back.

Wise Guy

Apes and monkeys are known for their intelligence. Next to people, gorillas and chimpanzees are thought to be the smartest of all animals.

Handy Thumb

Trying to pick up a pencil using only your fingers, not your thumb, is difficult. Using your thumb makes it easier, because it can press against the fingers like a clamp. Apes and monkeys have opposable thumbs, too, which help them to groom, pick leaves, and climb trees.

Bears

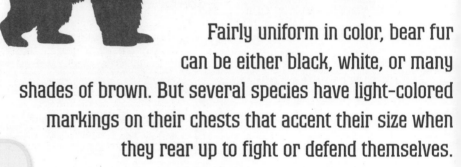

Fairly uniform in color, bear fur can be either black, white, or many shades of brown. But several species have light-colored markings on their chests that accent their size when they rear up to fight or defend themselves.

NEARSIGHTED

Bears are built for seeing small things close at hand, such as berries and other food. Sometimes they get so absorbed in eating that they don't see an approaching person. Hikers often whistle or wear bells to alert bears of their presence.

Spectacled Bear

The spectacled bear is the only bear that lives in South America. This unique creature, which gets its name from the markings around its eyes, roams along the Andes Mountains.

Bear-y Diverse

With its powerful body, the North American black bear can outrun a person, shimmy up a tree with amazing speed, and easily break through dense underbrush in a forest. Although called a black bear, it comes in many colors, such as blue-black, brown, cinnamon, or even white.

Sun Bear

The sun bear gets its name from the white or yellow marking on its chest, which resembles the rising sun. Sun bears are called *basindo nan tenggil* in the Malay language, which means "he who likes to sit high."

Nosing Around

Smell is probably a bear's greatest sense. Like a bloodhound, it can accurately sniff out a trail where prey walked many hours before. It can also pick up a scent from the air and find the source miles away.

KILLER CLAWS

A bear's foot comes equipped with five long, curved claws which are used to mark or climb trees, dig for food, excavate their dens, rip apart prey, scratch, or defend themselves.

FAST FEET

They may look slow and clumsy, but bears walk like people—on the soles of their feet, with heels touching the ground. Some are also fast runners. Brown bears can reach speeds of up to 40 miles per hour—faster than any Olympian sprinter and as fast as a greyhound!

Birds of Prey

Fine Feathers

Feathers do many jobs for birds of prey: Soft down keeps the birds warm. Strong wing feathers allow the birds to control flight, and tail feathers steer and brake. The flight feathers on the wings of many owls, including this great horned owl, have soft edges that make flight silent.

BIG AND LITTLE

Raptors come in all sizes. Biggest of them all, the Andean condor may weigh 25 pounds and have wings stretching to over 10 feet. It's about 250 times heavier than the smallest bird of prey, the tiny Asian falconet.

SIMPLY BIRDS

Not all birds that eat other animals are called birds of prey. Birds like the heron, above, do not have the same kind of bodies or hunting methods that other birds of prey do.

WONDER WINGS

Raptors that spend lots of time soaring have long, broad wings. Birds, like this turkey vulture, that catch rising air currents can cruise for hours and barely flap their wings. Soaring saves a lot of energy. Falcons, on the other hand, are fast-flapping flyers. Their narrow, pointed wings enable them to maneuver easily.

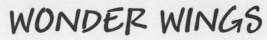

TOP OF THE HEAP

Raptors, such as this martial eagle, sit at the top of the food chain. Raptors hunt other animals, but almost nothing else hunts them. Their only enemies are other birds of prey and humans.

Talons of Doom

A raptor's talon-tipped feet are its most important weapon. Some fish-eating raptors, such as this osprey, have specially curved claws and spiny bumps on their feet to help them hook and hang on to their wriggling catch.

EAGLE EYES

Birds of prey have eyesight that is at least two to three times better than ours. Some can see a grasshopper from 100 yards away—the length of a football field! Eagles, like this golden eagle, can spy prey from over a mile away.

Africa

ID, Please
Zebra stripes are like human fingerprints—no two are exactly alike.

Room for More
Giraffes are ruminants, which means they have more than one stomach. They actually have four.

Can You Hear Me?
African elephants communicate with a frequency that cannot be heard by humans.

CAPE ANGER

Surprisingly calm-looking, the four-legged giant known as the Cape buffalo is actually quite dangerous. The sight or smell of a predator angers the Cape buffalo. It charges, unafraid, to protect its herd, which is enough to scare off the most dangerous predators—even the lion.

GIRLS RULE

LIONESSES ARE BETTER HUNTERS THAN MALE LIONS.

LONG NECK

Believe it or not, the giraffe has the same number of bones in its neck as most other mammals. A male giraffe can be up to 18 feet tall, have a 15-inch-long tongue, and reach high into acacia trees for its leafy meals.

With the Band

Zebras' stripes protect them from predators. When zebras are in a herd, the stripes blend together and make it hard for a predator to pick out only one.

43

Backyard Buddies

Chubby Cheeks

Chipmunks chatter, chirp, and whistle, but their high-pitched "chip-chip" gave them their name. Chipmunks spend their days stuffing their cheek pouches with seeds, nuts, and fruit. A chipmunk can hold up to four nuts in each chubby cheek pouch!

House Mouse

The house mouse will chew, suck, and eat almost anything, carefully clenching its mea[t] in its front paw and gnawing with sharp fron[t] teeth. Mice love grains, but they'll also eat strings, paper, and even cable wire!

Tall Tails

The gray squirrel has a big, bushy tail that helps it move, maintain balance, stay warm, and even communicate. When a squirrel senses an enemy, it flashes its tail to warn other squirrels. When a squirrel falls from a tree, the tail acts like a parachute. In the rain, the tail is an umbrella!

Boxing Bunnies

Hares are oversized rabbits, equipped with long ears, very thick fur, and strong hind legs that help them run up to 35 miles an hour and jump 6½ feet high! Male brown hares have an interesting way of winning a female's affection: They play-fight another male, chasing, kicking, and "boxing," until one of them gives up.

Fun Facts about RABBITS

Rabbits are crepuscular, which means they are most active at dawn and dusk.

Baby rabbits are born blind.

In southern Japan, there is an island populated by hundreds of friendly rabbits that will swarm people for food.

Cottontail rabbits molt twice a year.

Cuddly cottontail rabbits may look cute hopping around your yard, but they do something you may think is disgusting—they eat their own droppings! Actually, the bunny is being healthy, because its body gets more nutrients when its food is digested twice.

Getting Fishy

Swim, Fish, Swim!
There are at least 30,000 species of fish—more than any other kind of vertebrate.

Sensitive Nose
A fish "sniffs" by pulling water through the openings on its snout into a space above its jaw filled with chemical-sensing nerves.

Changing Temperature
Fish are cold-blooded. Their blood temperature changes with the temperature of the surrounding water. Fish like this perch can live in a warm lake in summer and stay in that same ice-covered lake in winter.

There and Back Again

Freshwater or saltwater? Some fish, like this sockeye salmon, go from one to the other.

Disguises

Some fish use disguises to hide from their enemies or to catch their prey. Color and shape are the most important parts of a fish's camouflage: The right combination can make a fish look like a rock, a plant, or part of a bigger fish! The leafy sea dragon has floating strands of skin that look like the seaweed it swims near.

WATER WAYS

Fish live in all kinds of water: warm and cold, fresh and salty, shallow and deep, near the shore, and in the open ocean. Different kinds of fish have adapted to each of these environments.

Fun Facts
about
Polar Bears

Adult male polar bears grow up to weigh as much as 1,600 pounds and rely on sea ice to hunt and catch their prey. Using its powerful jaws, a polar bear can instantly grab a seal with its sharp, pointed teeth, and haul it out of the water.

Polar bears only live near the Arctic ice cap—one of the coldest places on earth!

Polar bears' fur camouflages them in snow, but under their fur, they have black skin that soaks up the sun to help keep them warm.

Polar bears have no natural enemies in the wild. This means no other animals kill polar bears for food.

Polar bears have an excellent sense of smell, which helps them find their favorite food—seals.

Unlike most bears, polar bears do not hibernate, but mother polar bears will dig dens in the snow to keep their cubs safe and warm.

Pair Matching
Polar Bear Twins

There are 3 sets of polar bears below. Draw a line to connect the polar bear on the left with its identical twin on the right.

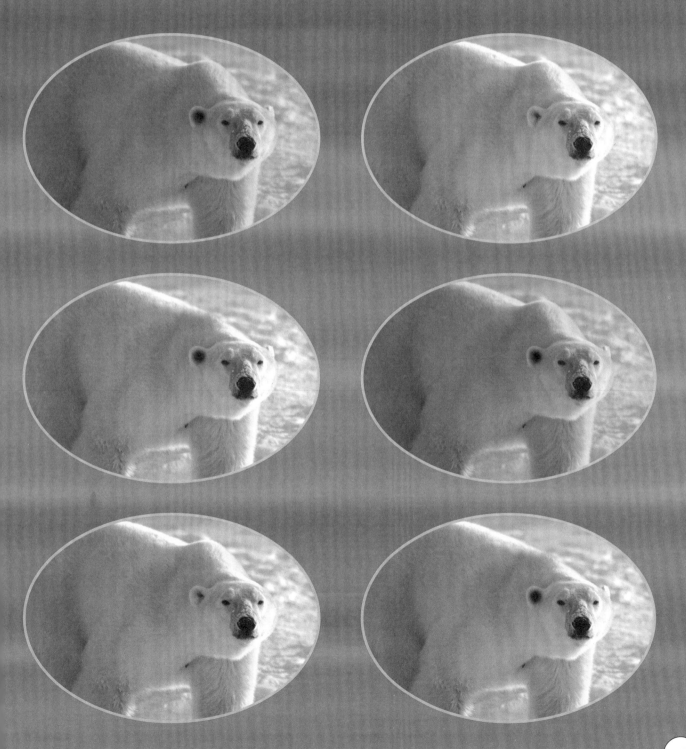

Farm Feathers

DID YOU KNOW?

A male chicken is called a rooster. A young female chicken is called a pullet until she lays her first egg, usually at about five months old. Then she is called a hen. A baby chicken is called a chick.

IF A HEN DOES NOT HAVE A BALANCED DIET, SHE MAY LAY EGGS WITH SOFT SHELLS.

Keep 'Em Coming

Hens lay eggs, but not all eggs will hatch into fuzzy, yellow chicks. The eggs need to be fertilized before they can hatch into babies. Hens can live up to 20 years and will lay eggs their entire lives!

COCK-A-DOODLE-DOO!

This is the early morning wake-up call made by roosters on farms around the world. Unlike female chickens, roosters do not lay eggs. Roosters scratch and claw the ground looking for food.

ALL CHICKENS HAVE A GOOD SENSE OF HEARING, BUT A POOR SENSE OF SMELL AND TASTE.

The red flap of skin under a rooster's beak is called a wattle. Have you ever seen a rooster waddle over to show off his wattle?

CHICKENS ARE THE WORLD'S MOST COMMON SPECIES OF BIRD.

Crocodilians

Alligators, crocodiles, gharials, and caimans belong to a group of reptiles known as crocodilians. These highly intelligent creatures lived alongside the dinosaurs, but—unlike those now-extinct animals—they were able to adapt to Earth's changes and survive.

Watery Living

Crocodilians are built for a life in and around water. They are strong swimmers, propelling themselves forward with their powerful tails. Their long, sleek bodies never stop growing and are protected by hard bony scales. When floating, the eyes, ears, and nostrils are exposed above water, but when underwater—where they can remain for over an hour—transparent shields slide across their eyes to protect them.

CROCODILE COUSINS

One way to tell alligators and crocodiles apart is by looking at their heads and jaws. An alligator has a rounded snout at the end of a slightly shorter head. A crocodile's head is longer and more triangular. When a crocodile closes its mouth, the larger teeth on its bottom jaw rest in spaces on the outside of its upper jaw. In an alligator's mouth, they rest on the inside of the jaw.

Caimans

Caimans, living in Central and South America, are closely related to alligators. Alligators are found only in the southeastern part of the United States and China.

Gharials

The Indian gharial has a long, slender snout and a bulb-like nose. Unlike other crocodilians, all of its sharp teeth—about 160 of them—are the same size. Gharials can grow to 20 feet long. Though fierce-looking, the endangered gharial is really quite shy and timid.

Marsupials

Marsupials are mammals that give birth very early and whose young must latch on to their mothers to finish developing. Females of most marsupial species have pouches to carry their babies for this reason.

All in the Family

There are four species of kangaroo: red kangaroo, eastern grey kangaroo, western grey kangaroo, and antilopine kangaroo, also called a wallaroo or wallaby. The tree kangaroo belongs to the same family but a different genus. It more closely resembles the kangaroo's possum-like ancestor.

Hop to It

Kangaroos can hop 30 feet and travel more than 30 miles per hour. Kangaroos cannot walk backwards.

Overhead Hoppers

The tree kangaroo is good at leaping from one tree to another, but it is rather clumsy on the ground. Compared to its ground-dwelling relatives, it has short back legs, but its long tail helps it stay balanced in the branches.

Sleepyhead

The Australian koala bear is a marsupial and not a member of the bear family. Koalas sleep for around 20 hours a day. They are able to eat eucalyptus leaves, which are poisonous to other animals, because bacteria in their stomachs breaks down the toxins. Koalas often get all the water they need from these leaves.

Woolly Matters

SHEEPISH

Sheep can be black, white, brown, or even spotted. Female sheep are called ewes, males are bucks or rams, and baby sheep are lambs, lambkins, or cossets.

Goat of Many Colors

There are many different kinds of goats, and each breed is unique. Some goats have horns, and some don't. Some have curly hair, and some have straight hair. They come in a variety of sizes and a number of colors—black, white, red, brown, spotted, and multicolored. Dairy goats provide milk that can be used to make cheese, yogurt, butter, ice cream, and even candy!

A MALE GOAT IS CALLED A BILLY.

A FEMALE GOAT IS CALLED A NANNY OR A DOE.

Woolly

Sheep's wool is the most commonly used fiber in the world. Can you think of something you have that is made from wool?

BAA! BAA! BAA! BAA!

The "baa, baa" sound a sheep makes is called bleating. A baby sheep can find its mother because it recognizes the sound she makes.

MOTHER SHEEP OFTEN GIVE BIRTH TO TWINS.

Stay Sharp?

Almost all goats naturally have two horns. Sometimes the horns of farm goats are removed so people and other animals won't get hurt by them.

A BABY GOAT IS CALLED A KID.

A group of goats is called a trip. A group of sheep can be called a trip, drift, drove, flock, herd, or mob.

57

Fun Facts about SIZE

Hummingbirds are the smallest birds in the world.

An ostrich's eye is bigger than its brain.

Komodo dragons are the largest lizards in the world. They can grow up to 10 feet long!

A leopard's tail is about as long as its body.

The sun bear is the smallest of the bears—about 3 to 4½ feet long and 100 pounds.

An elephant's toenail is as big as a human hand.

When it is born, a baby panda is smaller than a mouse.

Dogs and Cats

BEST FRIENDS

In the United States, there are about 74 million pet dogs and 88 million pet cats.

FEMALE CATS ARE CALLED
QUEENS.

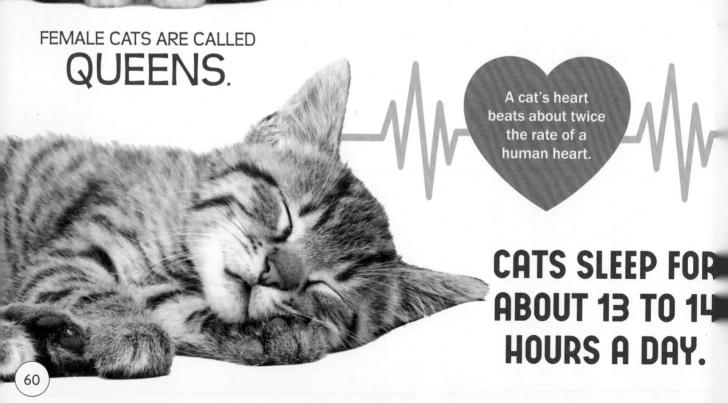

A cat's heart beats about twice the rate of a human heart.

CATS SLEEP FOR ABOUT 13 TO 14 HOURS A DAY.

Getting the Point

Dogs have developed the ability to understand human gestures. If a person points at something, a dog will look where the person is pointing. Other animals, including chimpanzees, will just look at the person's finger.

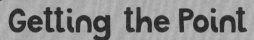

Dogs have great hearing! They can hear higher-pitched sounds than we can, like certain whistles.

A dog's nose is like a human's fingerprint: It is completely unique.

Dogs have around 1,700 taste buds, while cats only have around 475.

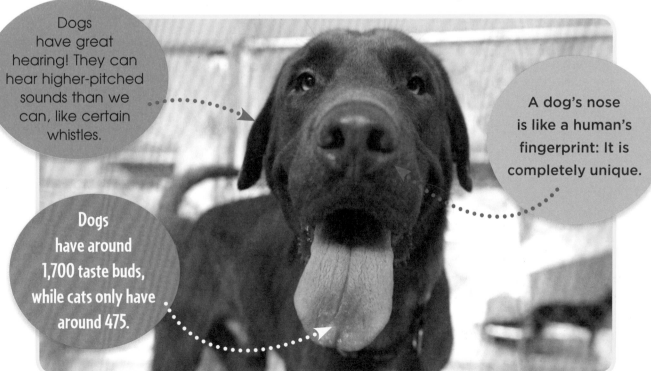

A Watery Life

Even though all mammals need to breathe air, many have evolved to spend their lives in or near water.

Think Pink

Largest of all river dolphins, the pink river dolphin of South America is about 7½ feet long and weighs up to 280 pounds. Baby river dolphins are dark gray. As they grow older, their skin lightens so that blood vessels beneath the skin can be seen, which gives them a pink coloring.

Brilliant Builders

At night, busy beavers gnaw on young trees, then haul, roll, or drag them downriver, their paddlelike tails helping them swim. Using stones, mud, and branches, these clever craftsmen construct dams.

DIP FROM DANGER

The capybara can weigh up to 140 pounds but is a strong swimmer. This South American rodent heads for water at the first sign of danger and can stay under for nearly five minutes to avoid a predator.

MERMAID MAMMALS

Sailors' tales of mermaids may have come from glimpses of manatees. These mammals, also called sea cows, live in shallow coastal waters and eat water plants and sea grasses. To deal with this tough food, manatees have intestines more than 145 feet long.

COOL TOOL

Webbed feet and a strong tail help the sea otter get around in the ocean. The otter sometimes places a flat rock on its chest and then pounds shellfish on it until the shellfish open.

Deep Dive

Before a harbor seal dives, it exhales as much air as it can, relying on oxygen stored in its muscle tissue and blood. Harbor seals slow their heart rates to three or four beats per minute while underwater, and their heartbeats speed up for a short time after they come up for air.

River Horse

Hippopotamuses leave the water only at night to eat grass and plants. Spending the day in the water keeps the hippos cool and comfortable.

Equine Elegance

The Equidae family consists of horses, zebras, and donkeys. Groups of wild horses and zebras are made up of mares, foals, and a male stallion that serves as the leader.

Sizing Them Up

Horses are divided into groups that indicate where the breed originated: hotbloods, coldbloods, and warmbloods. Some horses are from hot and humid environments. Others hail from lands with freezing temperatures. Warmbloods result from crossbreeding hotbloods and coldbloods.

Desert Dweller

African wild asses are about the same size as ponies, but they have shorter manes. They live in arid, hot, rocky deserts and can go for several days without water. They are not picky eaters either—they will eat any plants they can find!

A VANISHING BREED

The last herd of truly wild horses, called Przewalski's horses, was discovered in 1881 in the Gobi Desert in Mongolia. These horses were extinct in the wild until captive-bred individuals were reintroduced to Mongolia. As of 2014, there were close to 400 native-born and reintroduced Przewalski's horses in the wild.

Pony vs. Horse

The Shetland is the smallest pony, measuring 4 feet to the shoulder. The tallest horse, the Shire horse, can be more than 6 feet in height.

Adorable Animals

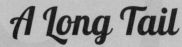

A Long Tail

Red pandas' bodies grow to be the size of a house cat, not including their big, bushy tails. A red panda's tail adds an extra 18 inches to its length.

TOP CLIMBER

Clouded leopards are among the best climbers of all cats! They can hang upside down from tree branches, and their rotating rear ankles let them climb headfirst down trees like a squirrel!

Fairy Tale

Little penguins, also known as little blue penguins and fairy penguins, are the smallest of the penguin species at around 1 foot tall and an average of 2 pounds. Their scientific name, *Eudyptula minor,* is well earned: It means "good little diver"! Unlike other penguins, these small seabirds have slate-blue feathers on their upper bodies instead of black. Fairy penguins are found in Australia, New Zealand, and nearby islands.

THE FENNEC FOX IS THE WORLD'S SMALLEST FOX, WEIGHING JUST A LITTLE OVER 2 POUNDS.

Nature's Pincushions

Hedgehogs have about 5,000 to 6,500 spines at a time. If it feels threatened, a hedgehog will curl into a prickly ball, tucking in its head, legs, and tail, discouraging predators from eating it. Hedgehogs generally sleep in this position.

Furry Friendly

Quokkas are marsupials, like kangaroos, that live in Australia. They are very friendly and often approach humans at campsites or cafés. However, human food isn't good for them—their diet is mostly made up of leaves and grasses.

LOVE BIRDS

In China and Korea, mandarin ducks are a symbol of faithfulness and love because they mate for life.

Winging It

With their awesome colors, shapes and sizes, butterflies and moths are some of the neatest insects around. You know it's summer when you see them floating over flower gardens, ponds, and fields.

Wild Beauties

There are more than 170,000 kinds of butterflies and moths. They live just about everywhere, from high mountain meadows and cold, windy tundra to tropical rain forests, deserts, and woodlands.

Moth or Butterfly?

How can you tell a moth from a butterfly? Moth antennae are lined with feathery hairs and have no club at the end; butterfly antennae have a small knob at the end. Moths rest with their wings out flat or angled like a tent; when butterflies rest, they fold their wings straight up.

1. New pupa

2. Chrysalis

3. Pupa nearing molt

4. Adult emerging

Complete Metamorphosis

The most advanced insects—such as butterflies, moths, bees, ants, and flies—undergo complete metamorphosis. They start as larvae (hatchlings), then go through a complete change. A caterpillar is a moth or butterfly larva. It turns into a pupa (1). Protected by a tough outer case called a chrysalis (2), the pupa forms legs, wings, and a new body (3). When the change is complete, the insect emerges as an adult—like this monarch butterfly (4)—looking very different from its younger self.

DANGEROUS COLORS

Most poisonous butterflies and moths have bright colors or large eyespots on their wings, warning signs that tell predators, "Danger! Stay away!" Some non-poisonous ones have the same patterns to make other animals think that they, too, are deadly!

SUPER SIPPERS

Adult moths and butterflies don't eat—they drink. They have a flexible, hollow tube, called a proboscis, for a mouth. They extend the proboscis into a flower's blossom, find the nectar, and drink it up—the way you use a straw.

Snakes

Now You See It... Now You Don't

Snakes use all kinds of ways to disguise themselves. The leaf-nosed snake has a head shaped like part of a tree, allowing it to blend in with its surroundings.

Snake Eyes

Snakes have no eyelids, so they always appear to be staring, even when they are sleeping. The clear lens, known as the spectacle, protects the eyes.

Reptile Rhino

Hornlike formations do not seem very snake-like, but the rhinoceros viper of Africa has them. This serpent has a blue-and-yellow butterfly design.

Snake Sense

Smell is a snake's most powerful sense. Using its forked, flicking tongue, a snake picks up microscopic particles from the air and ground. Because it is forked, the tongue can pick up a scent from more than one direction at a time.

HISSSSS!

The bull snake is one of the loudest hissing snakes. A very thin membrane in the front of its throat makes the sound possible. The snake opens its mouth wide and blows hard against this membrane, causing a nerve-shattering hiss.

Good Vibrations

Snakes have no outer ears to spoil their smooth outline. They "hear" you coming by sensing vibrations on the ground through their jawbones.

Food Chain
Herbivores

Herbivores are animals that eat plants. Some examples of herbivores are giraffes, hippos, and manatees.

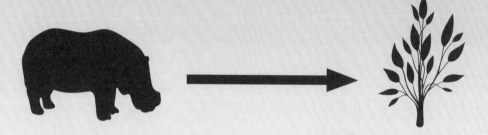

EAT TO LIVE

Plants can be low in nutrients that are necessary for an animal's energy, growth, and health, so some herbivores need to eat continuously to survive.

A Taste for Plants

Some herbivores only eat one kind of plant, while others, like the moose, eat a wide variety of them.

LEAFY DIET

Animals that eat mostly leaves, like pandas, caterpillars, and giraffes, are called folivores.

Sweet Tooth

Herbivores that eat mainly fruit are called frugivores. One example of a frugivore is the fruit bat.

Knock on Wood

Beavers are not xylophages, or animals that eat only wood. While wood is part of their diet, beavers also eat leaves, roots, and aquatic plants.

Oh, Deer!

Fallow deer often live in herds of more than 100 individuals.

Snow Shovel

All caribou antlers have a paddle at the front that allows them to scrape away snow and ice, just like a shovel!

THERE ARE MORE THAN 40 SPECIES OF DEER IN THE WORLD.

TOE THE LINE

Deer have four toes, but they only use their two big, central toes to walk. The two smaller, outer toes hover above the ground.

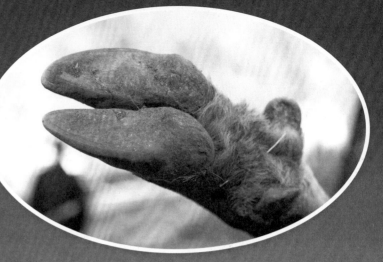

Jolly Good Fallow

Fallow deer, which can be found in Europe, Australia, the Americas, and Africa, can be recognized by their spots and flat antlers.

LONG WALK HOME

American caribou migrate the longest distance of any deer every year, in the spring and fall—over 400 miles in each direction!

In Danger

Endangered animals are groups of animals in danger of becoming extinct, or dying out.

Gorilla

These primates only travel about 400 yards per day. The group feeds at dawn, then moves into its nest of leaves and grass, where adults relax and youngsters play. They rise to feed in late afternoon, and return to their nest by sunset. Unfortunately, gorillas in the wild are threatened by habitat loss, poaching, or illegal hunting and capturing by humans, and disease.

MARKHOR

The markhor population is endangered due to hunters who kill the wild goats for their meat and horns.

Bengal Tiger

Like all tigers, this subspecies is endangered. There are only about 2,500 left in the world. Their population is in decline due to poaching to make products such as rugs, food, and Chinese medicine.

ASIAN ELEPHANT

At one time, Asian elephants roamed Asia from Syria to northern China. Today, nearly half of the remaining Asian elephants live in India. Elephants require a large area of natural range, which means they are one of the first species to be impacted when habitat is destroyed. Along with habitat loss, elephants are poached for the ivory trade and for their meat.

Tasmanian Devil

Tasmanian devils don't just exist in cartoons, but they are known for being fierce. Once at home all over Australia, the devils were reduced to living only on the island of Tasmania by farmers in the late 1800s. Devils are now protected by law, but they face a newer threat: a deadly cancer called Devil Facial Tumor Disease.

Okapi

The okapi is threatened by hunting and habitat loss in Africa. In 1952, conservationists set aside one-fifth of the Ituri Forest as a wildlife reserve. This allows scientists to study and protect the okapi and its natural habitat, which also protects other species that live there.

Camel Family

Camels, llamas, and alpacas all belong to the Camelidae family. Llamas and alpacas live in South America, while camels can be found in Asia and Africa.

UP HIGH

The llama lives on the slopes of South America's Andes Mountains. Its blood has a lot of red blood cells, which are very efficient at collecting oxygen. This enables the llama to cope with the lower oxygen levels found at high altitudes.

WORKLOAD

The people of the Andes have used llamas to carry heavy loads for thousands of years.

UNLIKE LLAMAS, ALPACAS ARE NOT USED AS PACK ANIMALS.

ONLY THE BEST

Baby alpaca fiber, also called cria fiber, is very expensive because it is so soft and lustrous.

In Fashion

Alpaca fleece comes in around 22 natural colors and is used to make textiles such as sweaters.

Built-in Shield

Camels have three eyelids on each eye— the third eyelid protects their eyes from the desert sand.

Camels can carry 400 pounds on their backs.

79

What a Hoot

Misnomer

The great horned owl does not have horns. It was named for the tufts of feathers that sit on either side of its head, resembling horns, called plumicorns.

Big Bite

Great horned owls prey on animals much larger than themselves, such as dogs, skunks, or falcons.

ODD OWL OUT

Unlike most owls, snowy owls are active during the day.

SNOWY OWLS SWALLOW THEIR PREY WHOLE.

Male snowy owls become whiter as they grow older.

Burrowing owls get their name because they live underground.

Day and Night

Most birds of prey are diurnal— active during the day. Most owls, however, are nocturnal. They do their hunting at night, relying on their hearing and low-light vision to locate prey.

Family Dynamics

SQUIRRELS WILL ADOPT THE ABANDONED BABIES OF THEIR RELATIVES.

At Home and On the Range

To feed her cubs, a mother cat has to kill at least three times as much prey as when she lives alone. Smaller cats, like this bobcat, bring rodents and other prey back to the den. Larger cats may take their youngsters along and have them practice their hunting skills.

LOVING PARENTS

The poison arrow frog carries its young to a nearby pool when the tadpoles are grown and ready to swim. When the parents and tadpoles reach the top of the rain forest trees, the parents let go of their young in the pools of water that form in certain plants.

The Littlest Cats

Except for lions, which live in groups, all young cats are cared for by their mothers alone. In the wild, cubs lead a dangerous life and must learn to hunt and fend for themselves before leading independent lives.

GETTING A GRIP

Children may claim that their parents are a pain in the neck, but not cats. Domestic and wild cats carry their young by the back of the neck—with no pain at all. Loose folds of skin on a kitten's neck are a natural handle. The lion cub, however, would rather hitch a ride on its mother's back.

Nests and Babies

Female crocodiles dig a hole into which they deposit their eggs before covering them with sand. Alligators prepare rounded nests of mud and decaying vegetation above the ground. Both nests protect the eggs as the sun's warmth incubates them. Unlike most other reptiles, crocodilian mothers guard their nests and stay close to their babies after they are born.

Mother dogs are very protective of their puppies and care for them until they are old enough to live with a family.

Kangaroo moms keep their babies, called joeys, in a pouch on their bellies for about 10 months.

Home in the Himalayans

TOUGH GUYS

The male Himalayan tahr has a mane that he can raise during mating season to intimidate competing males. Males lose a lot of weight during this time from all the fighting they do to win mates!

GIANT PANDA

The giant panda makes its home in the high mountains of central China, where bamboo is plentiful. The rare panda is confined to an area only 300 miles long and about 80 miles wide.

All Wrapped Up

Temperatures can get as low as -20°F in the winter, so snow leopards keep warm by wrapping their long, fluffy tails around their bodies like blankets.

WELL-DRESSED

Himalayan yaks have two layers of hair. The outer layer has long, waterproof hairs that keep the yak dry, and the inner layer is woolly and traps air to keep the yak warm.

Toothy Smile

Male musk deer do not have antlers. Instead, they grow canine teeth, called tusks, that can be close to 3 inches long.

Status Symbol

The colorful Himalayan monal is the national bird of Nepal.

Animal Babies

JOEYS, OR KANGAROO BABIES, ARE ABOUT THE SIZE OF A LIMA BEAN WHEN THEY ARE BORN.

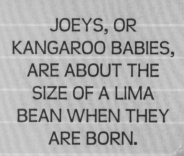

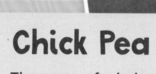

Chick Pea

The name of a baby peacock is a peachick.

PUPPIES ARE BORN BLIND, DEAF, AND TOOTHLESS.

Pup Love

Baby prairie dogs, otters, moles, and hamsters are called pups.

Little Flier

Bald eagle babies are called eaglets.

HOMEBODIES

Baby orangutans live with their mothers for seven to eight years. This is longer than any primate, other than humans.

87

Search & Find®
Prickly Situation

The porcupine may be slow and a little clumsy, but it has a unique way of protecting itself from predators. Once startled, a porcupine will prepare for attack by bristling up its 30,000 sharp spines, or quills, and stabbing the enemy with its dangerous points. The quills are released and embedded in the attacker, and the porcupine will regrow quills to replace lost ones.

There are 6 porcupines in the highlighted boxes. Can you find each one hidden among the other forest animals?

Animal Habitats
Desert

BORN TO RUN

Roadrunners are speedy on land, but they do not fly very well.

Deserts are the driest places on Earth.

What's That Smell?

A javelina is a piglike creature with sharp tusks. It exudes a skunky odor, making it easier for other javelinas to find it.

HOT SPOTS

The camel is built for life in the desert. Its body is very good at conserving water, and its long eyelashes protect its eyes from blowing sand. The pads of a camel's feet spread out to give it traction in the sand.

Fennec Family

Fennec foxes live in desert zones in the Sinai and Arabian peninsulas, and throughout the Sahara Desert in North Africa.

Thirsty?

Jerboas are small desert rodents that get all the moisture they need from their food. They don't drink any water!

Drink Up

Desert tortoises dig holes in the ground to catch rainwater. Once they've taken a long drink, desert tortoises can go up to a year without needing water again.

Neat Neighbors

MASSIVE MOOSE

Found in the northern United States, Canada, Europe, and Asia, moose often gather together during winter, feeding on bushes and willows, and sometimes wander into a backyard.

In Close Quarters

People in different parts of the world will find different animals in their backyards. If you live in Texas, you might look through the window to find a young green anole outside your house!

Real Stinkers

When a skunk is startled, it stamps its feet, turns its back, and raises its tail—and out squirts a horrible, stinking liquid! Skunks can fire six rounds of this putrid juice.

All Tucked In

Chipmunks prefer to live alone in burrows or holes called dens.

Planting the Seeds

Thousands of new trees grow every year because squirrels forget where they buried their acorns.

BASIC INSTINCTS

In the spring and fall, box turtles scavenge for food during daylight hours, and they sometimes lie out in the sun for warmth. In the summer, the turtles are most active in the morning.

ANCIENT ANIMAL

The bob-tailed Canadian lynx has been around for thousands of years. If you live in Canada or near the Northern Rockies, you might have this wildcat as your neighbor. The lynx crouches in trees, waiting to chase its next meal.

On the Menu

DID YOU KNOW?

INSECTS ARE A MAJOR SOURCE OF FOOD FOR MILLIONS OF DIFFERENT ANIMAL SPECIES.

FISH FOOD

Giant water bugs (seen below), caddis flies, mayflies, and other insects live in or around water. They make great meals for all kinds of fish, as well as for frogs, salamanders, snakes, and other animals that live in or close to streams and lakes.

BEAR FOOD

Can you believe that a grizzly bear would eat moths? Every summer in some areas of the Rocky Mountains, grizzlies feast on hordes of army cutworm moths, scooping them up in big bunches with their paws. The moths are around for only a few weeks, so the bears gobble up all they can!

Bird Food

Some swallows and warblers live on nothing but insects. It takes a lot of flies, gnats, and caterpillars to feed a nest of hungry babies, but there are always plenty of insects to go around!

BUG EAT BUG

What's on the menu? Other bugs! Ladybugs feed on aphids; hornets and wasps eat caterpillars; ants eat the larvae of beetles and termites; and dragonflies zoom around catching gnats and mosquitoes.

On Your Trail

When most ants leave the colony to search for food, they leave a scent trail. The ant touches its abdomen to the ground, releasing a chemical that other ants read with their antennae. Usually, the trail leads to a new source of food—or back home.

YOU AND ONLY YOU

The flower on a red clover is so big that most pollinators can't reach its nectar, but a bumblebee has the right stuff. Its massive body lets it burrow all the way in to collect pollen, which helps the clover reproduce.

Buzzing Backyard

Even the smallest patch of yard comes alive with the buzzing and chirping of insects as they fly about, crawl creepily, and simply hang out. These little critters are both pests and helpers to humans. What would a backyard be without them?

A CICADA CHORUS

The cicada has an amazing life cycle. Seventeen-year periodical cicadas live for 17 years as nymphs, the stage after hatching from eggs. When the whole population crawls above ground and becomes adults, they live for only a month, "singing," mating, and laying eggs. This buzzing chorus can be heard a mile away.

Fiery Fellows

Most ants are harmless, but the red fire ant bites and injects venom, causing a burning sensation. This native of Brazil came to the United States in the 1930s aboard ships. When they arrived, they multiplied and kept travelling.

OUT FOR BLOOD

Most people agree that mosquitoes are pests, but these bugs don't bite just to bother us. Although female mosquitoes eat nectar, they need blood to help their eggs develop. After drinking your blood, a female lays her eggs—up to 500 of them.

Fiddling Friends

You may not have ever seen a katydid—the green, long-legged relative of the cricket— but, chances are, you've heard one on a hot summer night. To attract females, males rub a sharp file on one wing against a scraper on the other wing, like a violinist moving a bow over a string. The raspy sound is music to female katydids.

Two-eyed Twigs

During the day, if you look closely in trees or shrubs, you just might spot a two-eyed twig! Stick insects avoid predators by sitting motionless. Usually long and thin, they are tree-brown, leaf-green, or any color that helps them blend into their background.

PEST CONTROL

Ladybird beetles, also known as ladybugs, provide pest relief to farmers and gardeners by preying on mealybugs, mites, and other plant-killing insects.

Animal Habitats
Wetlands

Wetlands are places that are filled or soaked with rain or seawater. Wetlands are home to a wide variety of amphibians, birds, and reptiles.

Rare Neighbors

American alligators are the primary hunters in Florida's Everglades swamp. Florida's Everglades is the only place in the world where alligators and crocodiles live side by side in the wild.

Big Blue Bird

The great blue heron is one of the largest herons in the world, with a wingspan of about 6 feet. Fish are this heron's main source of food, but it also eats rodents, lizards, and snakes. Great blue herons are common in North America, living near swamps, marshes, and sea coasts.

Wetland Wonderland

Pantanal (pictured here) is is one of the world's largest wetlands. Located in South America, it is home to over 600 types of birds, around 150 types of mammals, and more than 300 types of fish.

Speed Demon

The dragonfly is the fastest flier and has the keenest vision of any insect. It can see in almost every direction at once, and keeps its huge eyes clean by using special brushes on its front legs. Zooming after small insects, a dragonfly can hit 60 miles per hour.

Way Out West

ROCKY DWELLER

Bighorn sheep live throughout the Rocky Mountains in Canada, western and central United States, and northern Mexico.

ONE OF A KIND

Pronghorns look a lot like antelopes, so they are often called pronghorn antelopes or American antelopes. However, antelopes belong to the family Bovidae, while pronghorns are the only member of the Antilocapridae family. An antelope never sheds its horns, while pronghorns shed their horns each year.

Just Barking

Prairie dogs get their name from their doglike bark, but they're actually rodents! They live in communities called dog towns made up of hundreds of prairie dog families in networks of tunnels.

GO WEST
American bison, also known as buffalo, are considered an iconic, or recognizable, image of the Great Plains and the Old West.

PROCEED WITH CAUTION
Bison have an excellent sense of smell and great hearing, but they do not have very good eyesight. If a group, or herd, of bison is startled, it may stampede.

Need for Speed
The pronghorn is the fastest land mammal in North America and the second fastest land mammal in the world.

What's in a Name?

A group of rattlesnakes is called a rhumba or rumba.

A group of chickens is called a clutch, a brood, a peep, or a flock.

Kangaroos live in groups called mobs.

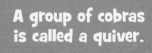

A group of cobras is called a quiver.

A group of pugs is called a grumble.

A group of porcupines is called a prickle.

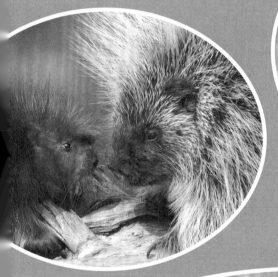

A group of tigers is called an ambush or streak.

A group of frogs is called an army.

Food Chain
Omnivores

Animals that eat both plants and other animals are called omnivores. Some examples of omnivores are coyotes, raccoons, and bears.

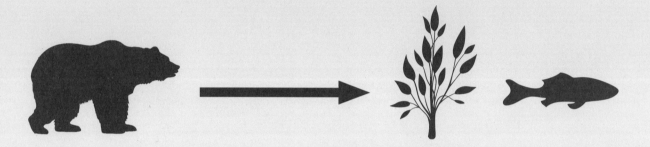

OMNIVORES CAN LIVE IN A WIDE RANGE OF HABITATS BECAUSE THEIR DIETS ARE MADE UP OF ANY EDIBLE FOOD THEY CAN FIND.

BEAR-Y LARGE

The largest terrestrial, or land-dwelling, omnivore is the Kodiak brown bear. It can grow up to 10 feet tall and weigh over 1,200 pounds. It eats grass, plants, fish, berries, and sometimes other mammals.

THE SMALLEST OMNIVORE IS THE PHARAOH ANT. ITS DIET INCLUDES EGGS, CARRION, INSECTS, NUTS, GRAINS, AND FRUIT NECTAR.

Omnivores like this raccoon have both sharp teeth to tear prey and large molars to help chew plants.

BIG DIET

At one time, people thought chimps were strictly plant eaters, but primatologist Jane Goodall discovered that chimps occasionally eat meat as well. They may eat ¼ pound of meat in one day when hunting, including meals such as monkeys, pigs, birds, and antelopes.

DID YOU KNOW?

Humans are omnivores!

Interesting Characteristics

Hippopotamuses secrete an oily red substance that acts as a sunblock.

Goldfish can lose their color when not exposed to enough light.

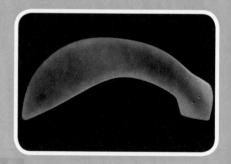

A puffin's feathers have special oils that make them waterproof.

If a certain type of worm, called the planarian, is split into pieces, each piece will turn into a whole new worm.

Beavers' teeth never stop growing. They gnaw on branches or sticks to keep their teeth from growing too long.

Ducks do not have nerves in their feet. If they're walking on land, they can't tell if the ground feels hot or cold.

Fill in the Blanks

Fascinating Animal Facts

Fill in the missing letters to complete the fun animal facts below.
Then write the numbered letters in order at the bottom of the
page to find out which animal no longer lives in the wild!

The smallest bird in the world is the

__ U __ M __ __ __ __ __ R D.
         1

The only relative of the giraffe is the

__ K __ __ I.
 2

An animal that is active at
night and sleeps during the day is

N __ C T __ __ __ A __.
        3

This animal is often known
as man's best friend:

__ O __.
 4

Ducks have no nerves in their

__ E __ T.
 5

Animals that have no backbone are called

__ N V __ T __ B R __ __ __ S.
 6

This animal makes its own natural sunscreen:

__ I __ __ O P __ T __ M __ S
                   7

Puffins have waterproof

__ E __ T __ __ R S.
    8

Answer: The __ __ __ __ __ __ __ __ !
       1 2 3 4 5 6 7 8

Spiders

Do Not Disturb

Imagine someone tearing down the walls of your room and carrying your possessions across town. Animals have living quarters, too. When you watch these creatures, try to be respectful of their space. Don't stand close to nesting birds, touch spider webs, or carry off rocks that serve as shelter.

At Home Anywhere

Spiders can live almost anywhere, in any climate! The only places they haven't been found are in oceans, extremely tall mountains, and polar regions.

THERE ARE THREE SPECIES OF BLACK WIDOW SPIDERS IN NORTH AMERICA: SOUTHERN, WESTERN, AND NORTHERN.

Wolf Pack

After her babies are hatched, a wolf spider carries them on her back for weeks while they develop.

ANCIENT ARACHNID

Daddy longleg spiders are ancient! Scientists have found fossils of these spiders that are 400 million years old.

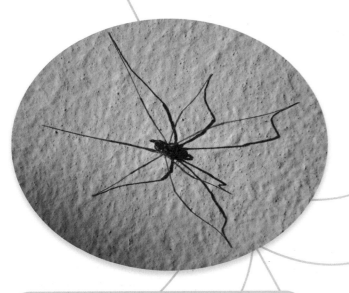

Roommates

House spiders are mainly found in the corners of rooms in our houses, especially hidden areas like basements or attics. They aren't poisonous, and their webs work to catch their favorite meal: insects!

COUNT TO SIX

Look at any kind of insect and you'll see six legs. Spiders, which have eight legs, are not insects (although they are related). They are called arachnids. Centipedes and millipedes look pretty buggy, too, but they have lots of legs—far too many to be insects.

Deadly Bite

The most poisonous spider in the world is the Brazilian wandering spider, because the poison from its bite can kill a human.

WHY IS THIS TARANTULA
NOT AN INSECT?
HINT: COUNT ITS LEGS!

Rainbow Bright

Beauty in Numbers

The nudibranch (NEW-dih-bronk), a type of snail, are abundant in shallow, tropical waters, but can be found throughout the oceans of the world. Their vivid colors make them some of the most beautiful creatures in the world!

Delightful Display

Male peacocks, rather than females, are the birds with the beautiful feathers. They use their tail feathers to get the attention of female peahens who will choose the peacock with the best display.

SLIMY STUNNER

Unlike most fish, mandarinfish don't have scales. Instead, they have slimy skin covered with mucus that makes them smell terrible! Their bright color warns predators that they will taste bad.

PRETTY DEADLY

The blue-ringed octopus is beautiful but deadly. It has venomous saliva which can paralyze and kill its prey— or even humans!

For Show

The lilac-breasted roller gets its name from its courtship flight to attract mates. It will fly to great heights and then make fast, shallow dives with a rolling or rocking motion, while crying loudly.

Clever Capture

The cuckoo wasp lays its eggs in the nests of other wasp species. Its larvae will wait until the host larvae have hatched and had a meal before the cuckoo wasps hatch and eat them!

RAINBOW BOAS GET THEIR COLOR FROM THEIR IRIDESCENT SCALES THAT REFLECT LIGHT TO CREATE A RAINBOW.

Asia

Spot-on Felines

The black panther is not a species, but a name that refers to any big cat born with black fur, such as black leopards. Black leopards and other wild black cats get their coloring from a gene that controls the amount of black pigment, or color, in the fur. These big cats have extra black pigment, which makes their coats completely black. Don't be fooled, though: Black panthers still have spots—they're just harder to see!

Bathing Beauties

Monkeys taking a bath? Not exactly. In the cold, snowy mountains of Japan, these macaques sit in hot springs just to get warm.

FRESH FOOD

The Asian giant hornet is an aggressive, predatory insect that attacks honeybees and uses their larvae as food for its young.

Good Day for a Mud Bath

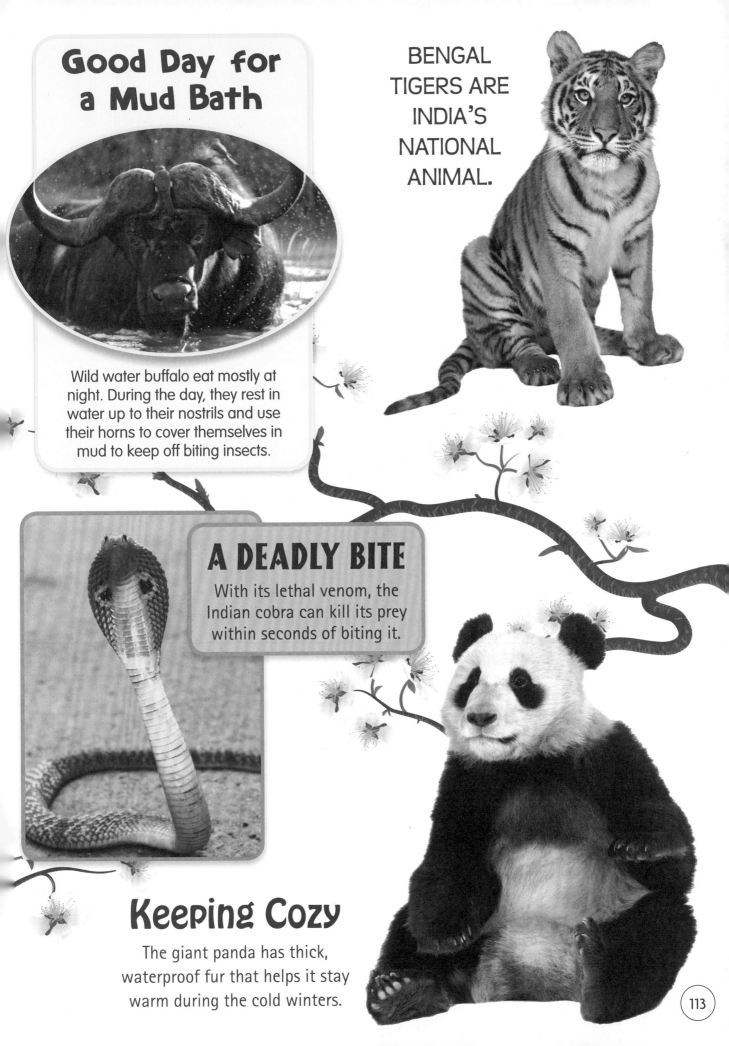

Wild water buffalo eat mostly at night. During the day, they rest in water up to their nostrils and use their horns to cover themselves in mud to keep off biting insects.

BENGAL TIGERS ARE INDIA'S NATIONAL ANIMAL.

A DEADLY BITE

With its lethal venom, the Indian cobra can kill its prey within seconds of biting it.

Keeping Cozy

The giant panda has thick, waterproof fur that helps it stay warm during the cold winters.

Masters of Deception

How to fool the enemy—that's a trick many lizards have mastered. In a world where most of the predators possess superior size, strength, and speed, lizards have become masters of illusion, deception, and trickery.

Freeze!

Chameleons know that sometimes it's better just to stand still when you want to escape a predator. A chameleon's color usually blends with its environment, making it doubly hard to spot. An attacker will often go right on by.

LIZARD BALL

If you can't run, and you can't hide, what's the next best thing? The armadillo lizard thinks that rolling into a ball and biting its tail is a good solution. By doing this, the heavily armored lizard protects its soft belly from an attacker, who finds the armadillo lizard's spiky armor as painful to bite as a cactus.

Distraction Tactic

Lizards have color for good reason. For the five-lined skink, its bright blue tail says, "Attack me!" Unlike the striped body, the tail attracts a predator's attention, and it can be discarded if necessary. Meanwhile, the skink escapes.

BLUE-TONGUED SKINKS GET THEIR NAME FROM THE BLUE TONGUE THEY STICK OUT TO SCARE AWAY PREDATORS.

Heads or Tails?

Sometimes two heads are better than one. The Australian shingleback's broad, stumpy head-shaped tail makes it appear to have two heads. This confuses its enemies, who prefer to attack the head directly from behind, giving the shingleback a 50-50 chance of escape.

Good Planning

A basilisk lizard knows how to take a nap. Living in Brazil's tropical rain forest, it crawls out to the tip of a thin branch that extends out over a small stream. When a hungry snake slithers too close, the branch shakes. With this warning, the basilisk drops into the water, safely out of the snake's reach.

HORNED LIZARDS SHOOT BLOOD FROM THEIR EYES TO PROTECT THEMSELVES.

Make Yourself Useful

Pollinators

Lots of plants reproduce by making flowers—but the flowers can't make seeds until they get pollinated. Bees, butterflies, moths, and some beetles are pollinators: When they visit a flower to eat, they get covered with pollen, a soft powdery substance. They spread it as they go from flower to flower.

Recyclers

Carrion beetles feed on yucky stuff, such as dead animals, fur, and feathers. They help prevent the spread of disease by turning waste materials into fresh new soil that is rich in nutrients. This helps plants grow, making food for other animals.

Got Silk?

Ever wonder why silk costs so much? It comes from specially bred and fed silkworms. Each silkworm cocoon is made of a single thread about 1,000 yards long. That thread must be carefully unwound and processed.

May I Help You?

Praying mantises help us out by doing what comes naturally—eating other bugs. The ones they like to eat are usually the same kinds that wreck crops and gardens.

Spot the Difference

Busy Bee

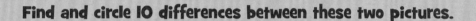

Find and circle 10 differences between these two pictures.

Answers on page 223

Spooky Names

No Bloodsuckers Here

Despite their name, dracula shrimp gobies are peaceful. These fish dig burrows in the sand and seldom stray far from their territory.

LITTLE BONES

Skeleton shrimp have see-through bodies, which is how they got their name. Skeleton shrimp are tiny—they only reach 1½ inches long!

Devilishly Sharp

The spikes on the thorny devil don't just warn away predators; they also collect water for the lizard to drink by directing the water towards its mouth.

SCARY SOUNDS

The death's-head hawk moth was named for the markings on its thorax, the area between the neck and abdomen, which look like a human skull! When the moth is disturbed, it makes an eerie squeaking sound.

Ghost in the Night

The ghost bat is Australia's biggest carnivorous bat and will swoop down and bite its prey behind the neck before carrying it back to the bat's perch to eat.

Underground Monsters

The Gila monster spends about 95% of its time underground and only emerges to eat and sunbathe. Gila monsters don't eat very often and can store fat in their tails.

Fun Facts about Red Pandas

Red pandas have caused debate among scientists trying to identify whether they are members of the bear family or the raccoon family. The answer? They belong to neither! Like giant pandas, red pandas eat bamboo and are native to the forests of Asia. However, they also live in parts of India, Tibet, and Nepal. Red pandas are most closely related to the group that includes raccoons and skunks, but they belong to their own independent family called Ailuridae.

They are most active at dawn and dusk.

A red panda can curl itself into a ball when it gets cold. In warm weather, it stretches out on a branch and pants to cool its body temperature.

Baby red pandas stay with their mothers for about a year before they are able to live on their own.

Dolphins

UNDERWATER EARS

Although they have no ears on the outside of their heads, whales and dolphins have excellent hearing. Tiny pinholes, as narrow as a pencil, are located just behind their eyes. Through these holes, they can pick out sounds from many miles away.

Motherly Love

Because they are mammals, mother dolphins nurse their babies and take care of them. A dolphin calf will often stay with its mother for three to six years.

Racing and Chasing

Dolphins like to swim fast. When a speeding boat passes by, they'll race out in front and ride its bow waves. When racing each other, they'll first leap into the air and then take off after hitting the water. Dolphins also play tag and dance on their tails across the water's surface.

Mongooses and More

Many members of the mongoose family, including the dwarf mongoose, banded mongoose, and meerkat, are native to Africa.

Safety in Numbers

Banded mongooses gather together and move as a group when they spot a predator approaching, creating the appearance of one large animal. Those at the front of the group may rear up on their hind legs and snap at the predator to scare it away.

Reporting for Duty

In a group of meerkats, one member will serve as the lookout, or sentry, and alert the others of danger if a predator is near. Meerkats will take turns keeping watch throughout the day.

Ladies First

Dwarf mongooses are a very social species. A group of dwarf mongooses can have up to 40 members, with a dominant female holding the highest rank. This female and her mate are usually the only members of the group to breed. The other adult mongooses help raise the young.

Playing Roles

While meerkat mothers forage, or search, for food, other male and female meerkats stay behind to babysit the young.

Nice Shades

Meerkats have dark patches around their eyes to help lessen the glare of the sun.

NO ONE SIZE FITS ALL

Different mongoose species come in a variety of sizes. The dwarf mongoose is around 7 to 10 inches in length, while the Egyptian mongoose, at left, can be up to 2 feet long.

Flying Colors

Moving In

Female golden-breasted starlings build nests inside tree holes abandoned by woodpeckers. This is where the starlings will lay their eggs.

Royal Standout

The common kingfisher is one of the most brightly colored birds in Europe.

The scarlet ibis is a South American shorebird named for its striking red feathers. This bird gets its color from the food it eats, which includes shrimp and crabs. Flamingos get their color the same way: The shrimp and algae they eat turn their feathers pink.

Nature's Heater

The female emerald starling has a featherless spot called a brood patch on her stomach to help transfer body heat to her eggs.

Gather Together

As many as thousands of scarlet ibises may live together in a colony, which helps them to keep watch for predators.

Dimorphic Birds

What does it mean to be dimorphic?

A dimorphic species is a species in which males and females differ in appearance. Many species of birds are dimorphic, including peacocks, fairy bluebirds, and lesser green broadbills.

Male peacocks have brilliant green and blue feathers, while female peahens are mainly brown with green feathers only at the neck.

Female fairy bluebirds are covered in soft blue feathers, and male fairy bluebirds have bright blue and black feathers.

The male lesser green broadbill has vivid green feathers, black bands across his wings, and a black dot behind each ear. The female has duller green feathers and no black markings.

Fun Facts about Basilisks

These reptiles can run about 20 feet on the water before they start to sink, but they are also very good swimmers and can stay underwater for 30 minutes.

The basilisk lizard is also known as the Jesus lizard.

Basilisk lizards live in tropical rain forests in Mexico, South America, and Central America.

The green basilisk lizard can walk on water using special folds of skin on its back feet that spread out to create a paddle.

The basilisk lizard eats insects, flowers, fruit, small rodents, worms, and other lizards.

Jungle Maze

Going Bananas

Time for a snack! Follow the maze to help the monkey reach the bananas.

FINISH

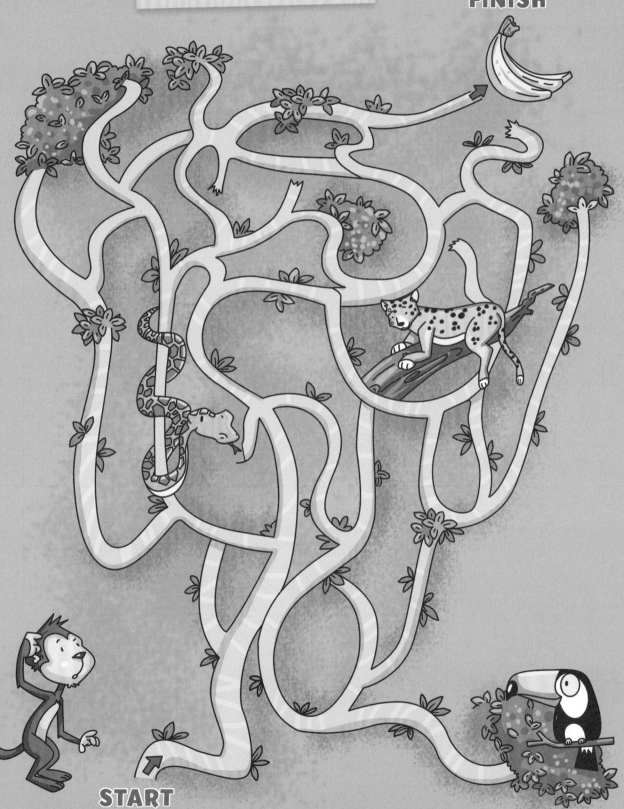

START

Rodents

FATTENING UP

Woodchucks, also known as groundhogs and whistle pigs, hibernate, or sleep, during winter. In summer months, they eat plenty of food, gorging themselves on plants and sometimes vegetables from your garden.

BUNDLED UP

Chinchillas have thick, soft fur that protects them from cold temperatures in the Andes Mountains where they live.

CHINCHILLAS CAN JUMP UP TO 6 FEET IN THE AIR.

Worth Their Salt

Porcupines love salt, and often gnaw on tools that have been held by sweaty palms.

Wild vs. Tame

Guinea pigs are members of a family of rodents called cavies. They are popular pets all over the world. Wild cavies mainly live in grasslands in South America. Domestic guinea pigs have been bred in a variety of colors, but wild cavies have short gray or brown fur.

CHINCHILLAS ARE MATRIARCHAL, MEANING THE FEMALES ARE THE LEADERS OF THE GROUP.

Make a Lake

By building dams, the beaver raises the water level around its home, or lodge, which keeps the entrance underwater. The beaver uses the pond created by the dam to store branches and other food for the winter.

DID YOU KNOW?

Many people think ferrets are rodents, but they are actually a member of the weasel family!

Fun Facts about
Farm Animals

Hens lay different colored eggs, from white to brown to green to pink to blue.

Chickens are the closest living relatives of the T-Rex.

Different types of cows make different kinds of milk.

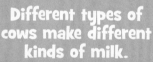

There are over 1 billion cows in the world.

Roosters can fly, but not very far because they're so heavy.

It is physically impossible for pigs to look up at the sky.

A horse's eyes are nine times larger than a human's. They have the largest eyes of any land mammal.

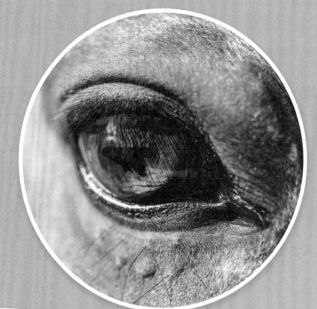

Chickens have more bones in their necks than giraffes.

A sheep doesn't have any front teeth on the upper jaw.

Cows may have different accents depending on where they live.

Worldwide, more people eat and drink milk products made from goats than any other animal.

Cultural Significance

SOUL SEARCHING

The Aztecs used to bury Chihuahuas with the dead, as they believed the dogs had the power to guide human souls through the underworld.

Queen of the Nile

Cats descended from the African wild cat and began living with humans in Egypt about 4,000 years ago. Egyptians considered them sacred and worshipped them in the form of a goddess that had the head of a cat.

PICTURE PERFECT

Early people hunted horses for food and their sturdy hides. Scientists have found early cave drawings depicting horses.

War Horses

For 5,000 years, through World War I, humans used horses to assist them in wars. Riding without saddles, ancient warriors battled their enemies. In the Middle Ages, knights rode into battle on horses that were as heavily armored as they were.

Getting Together

Dogs and humans have lived side by side for more than 15,000 years. Most likely, this relationship began when wild dogs started looking for food near human settlements. As the animals grew tamer, people started to keep them as pets. Dogs are considered to be man's best friend because they provide great companionship.

CHARIOT RACE

Of all domesticated animals, the horse was one of the last to be tamed by humans. Before they were ever ridden, horses and donkeys were trained to pull carts and chariots. The ancient Greeks and Romans used horses for chariot racing, which was first staged at the Olympic Games in 680 B.C.

Fun Facts about Sea Creatures

Octopuses have three hearts.

This fierce, male stickleback, 2 to 4 inches long, builds a nest for his fry (young fish) and keeps them there. He tries to keep the babies from wandering off and may bring them back in his mouth. After about two weeks, the nest is worn out and so is dad.

A blue whale's tongue can weigh as much as an elephant.

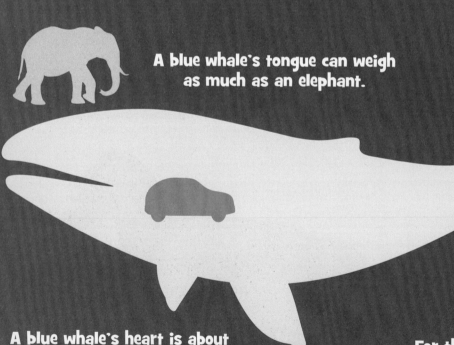

A blue whale's heart is about the size of a small car.

For the first year of its life, a baby blue whale gains about 200 pounds every day.

Shark scales are different than other fish scales. Called denticles, shark scales are constructed like very hard, sharp teeth. Shark skin is like a spiky suit of armor—you can be injured just by touching it.

BEFORE

All puffer fish are slow and clumsy swimmers, making them seem like easy prey.

AFTER

After a few quick gulps, this puffer balloons up to three times its normal size. Take that, predator!

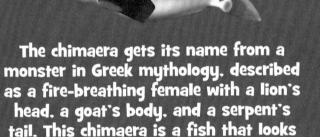

The chimaera gets its name from a monster in Greek mythology, described as a fire-breathing female with a lion's head, a goat's body, and a serpent's tail. This chimaera is a fish that looks like it has a rat's tail, a rabbit's teeth, a mammal's nostrils, fin spines like a porcupine, and wings like a bird.

The giant squid, which may grow to more than 40 feet long, has the biggest eyes of any living creature.

South America

ON GUARD

Some farmers use llamas to guard their sheep.

Above It All

Emerald tree boas live their entire lives in trees, only moving to the ground to get to another tree.

The tapir has a trunk like an elephant that it uses to pull leaves off of trees and pluck fruit from bushes and branches.

FLAMINGOS EAT WITH THEIR HEADS UPSIDE DOWN.

ARMORED UP

In Spanish, *armadillo* means "little armored one." All armadillo species except the nine-banded armadillo live in Latin America.

CAPYBARAS ARE THE WORLD'S LARGEST RODENT.

Fun Facts about Gazelles

Gazelles can be found energetically bouncing up and down on all fours when they feel threatened. This movement is called stotting or pronking.

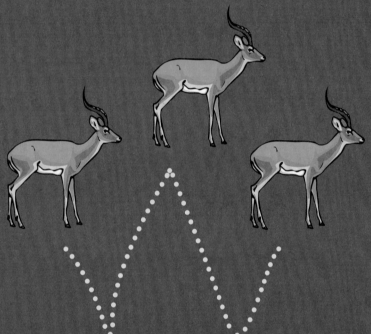

Dama gazelles sometimes stand on their hind legs to eat from acacia trees and various plants up to 6 feet high!

The dama gazelle is the largest and tallest species of gazelles.

Gazelles rely on their speed to protect them from attacks by predators such as lions and cheetahs.

Secret Science Code

The Name Game

To help scientists identify animals, they give each animal a two-part Latin name. The first word in its name is the genus that animal belongs to, and the second word represents its species.

Use the key below to crack the code and find out the Latin names of these gazelles!

A = 1 C = 2 D = 3 E = 4 G = 5 H = 6 I = 7
M = 8 N = 9 O = 10 R = 11 S = 12 T = 13 U = 14

The dama gazelle is known to scientists as

$$\frac{}{9}\ \frac{}{1}\ \frac{}{9}\ \frac{}{5}\ \frac{}{4}\ \frac{}{11}\ \ \frac{}{3}\ \frac{}{1}\ \frac{}{8}\ \frac{}{1}.$$

Thomson's gazelle is called

$$\frac{}{4}\ \frac{}{14}\ \frac{}{3}\ \frac{}{10}\ \frac{}{11}\ \frac{}{2}\ \frac{}{1}\ \frac{}{12}$$

$$\frac{}{13}\ \frac{}{6}\ \frac{}{10}\ \frac{}{8}\ \frac{}{12}\ \frac{}{10}\ \frac{}{9}\ \frac{}{7}\ \frac{}{7}.$$

Handling the Heat

Each of these species has its own way of dealing with the high temperatures that come with desert life.

Bactrian camels have two humps that store fat as energy and water. To protect the Bactrian camel's nose and eyes from the blowing sand, its nostrils close and its eyebrows and eyelashes act like curtains over its eyes.

Light Appetite

If a scorpion can't find food, it can slow its metabolism so much that it can survive by eating just one insect per year!

Fennec foxes get most of their water from the food they eat.

Double Defense

Regal horned lizards can change their color to blend in with their surroundings to avoid predators, but if that doesn't work, they can inflate until they seem too big to eat!

Come on Down

To avoid the high temperatures of the desert, desert tortoises burrow underground in tunnels that can be up to 32 feet long with up to 25 tortoises in each shelter.

And They're Off!

Black-tailed jackrabbits avoid predators by leaping up to 10 feet and running up to 40 miles per hour in a zigzag pattern.

Animal Habitats
Coral Reef

Coral reefs are actually made up of tiny animals called polyps that eat smaller, floating sea creatures by catching them with their tentacles.

EASY BEING GREEN

Scientists believe that the green sea turtle gets its color from its diet of seaweed and sea grass.

In the Band, Out of the Water

The banded sea krait lives most of its life in the water, but lays its eggs on land.

Walk on By

When manatees are in shallow water, they use their flippers to walk by, slowly placing one in front of the other.

Lots of Limbs

Most sea stars have five arms, but some can grow as many as 40!

CELL FOOD

A sea sponge doesn't have tissues or organs. Instead, each individual cell digests its own food!

Freshwater Life

Freshwater animals live in lakes, ponds, rivers, or streams. These bodies of water don't have much salt in them, so different animals live there than in the salty ocean.

SURPRISING SPEED

Hippopotamuses don't normally move very fast, but they can reach speeds of 30 miles per hour in short bursts!

Kiddie Meal

It's dangerous to be a young American alligator—adult alligators are known to prey on them for food!

BUILT FOR THE RIVER

Pink river dolphins, also known as botos, live in the Amazon River and have special adaptations that make them very different from the dolphins that live in the ocean. They are only distantly related.

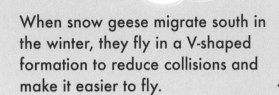

When snow geese migrate south in the winter, they fly in a V-shaped formation to reduce collisions and make it easier to fly.

Go with the Flow

Some animals that live in rivers or streams, like this beaver, have special adaptations that let them live in flowing water. Other freshwater animals live better in still waters, like ponds or lakes.

The American alligator can grow up to 15 feet in length.

Piranhas have large, sharp teeth that are used to slice through prey, like other fish and occasionally land animals in the water.

Animal Habitats
Rain Forest

Going Green

Sloths move so slowly that sometimes algae grows on their fur.

Colorful Creatures

Scarlet macaws are extremely colorful parrots that live in the top layer of the rain forest, called the emergent layer. Macaws mainly eat fruit, nuts, and seeds.

TOTALLY TROPICAL

From treetop to jungle floor, 40 square miles of rain forest may hold 125 kinds of mammals, along with many other animals. The jaguar—the largest cat found on the American continents—lives in the tropical forests of South America.

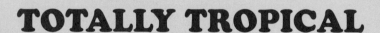

Rain forests are regions with wet, hot climates. They're divided into four layers from top to bottom: emergent, canopy, understory, and forest floor. Each layer has a different amount of rain and sunlight and different types of animals and plants.

DID YOU KNOW?

TWO OF A KIND

Marmosets and tamarins are among the few monkeys or apes that commonly give birth to twins.

A toucan's beak isn't dangerous at all! Toucans use their bills as a feeding tool—kind of like their own knife and fork. They can peel fruit and reach with their beaks to grab other treats, such as insects, eggs, and lizards.

Out on a Limb

In the dense canopy of Brazil's rain forest, the golden lion tamarin eats, sleeps, and travels. To avoid predators, most forest-dwelling monkeys, such as tamarins and marmosets, sleep in the hollows of trees—a tough spot for a jaguar to reach. Golden lion tamarins are named for their thick golden fur, which resembles a lion's mane.

All About Bats

There are over 1,000 bat species in the world that fall into two categories: microbats and megabats.

BLOODSUCKERS

The vampire bat hunts warm-blooded prey like birds, cows, or horses. It lands near its prey and creeps up behind it before sinking its teeth in to drink its blood.

Not Listening

Megabats, like this flying fox, eat mainly fruit. Since they don't need to listen for their food, they have smaller ears than microbats.

Bats are the only mammals that can truly fly—all the others simply glide.

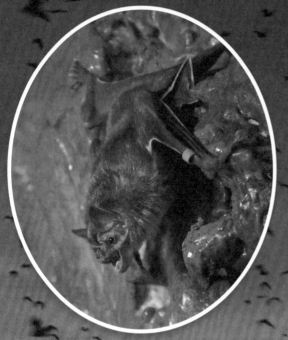

SNEAKING A SNACK

Vampire bats can drink blood from their prey for more than 30 minutes before the animal notices.

Most microbats eat flying insects that they catch after dark, but some eat lizards, frogs, and fish.

Antler Parade

LARGE AND IN CHARGE

Who is that giant deer? It's a moose, the largest member of the deer family!

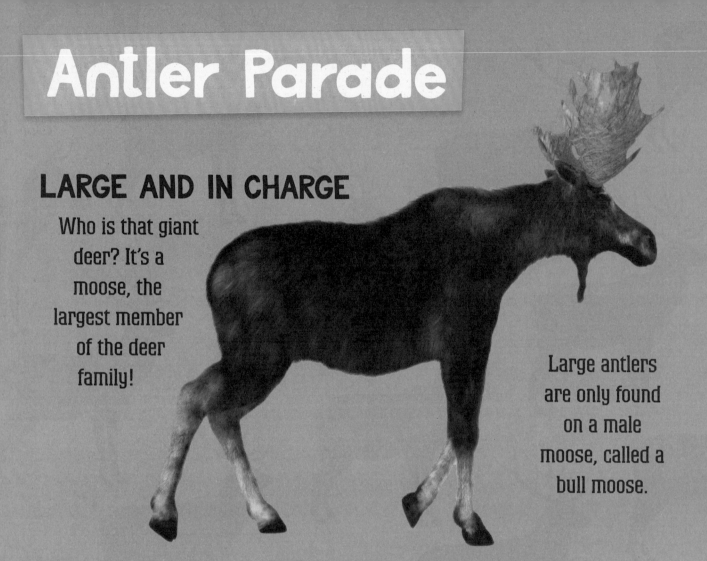

Large antlers are only found on a male moose, called a bull moose.

ANTLERS FOR ALL

Both male and female caribou grow antlers. Only males grow antlers in most other species of deer.

'Tis the Season

Reindeer change their eye color based on the season.

ON REPEAT

Elk are much larger than most of their deer relatives. The bull elk loses its antlers every year in March, and he begins to grow them back in May.

Head Start

A baby moose is called a calf. By the time a calf is five days old, it can run faster than a person.

Antarctica

Antarctica is the land on Earth's South Pole.
It is the coldest and driest continent on the planet.

BRR...IT'S COLD OUT HERE!

Animals can only come ashore along the coastline, because the mainland is freezing.

Wolves of the Sea

Orcas, also called killer whales, are the largest members of the dolphin family. They are sometimes referred to as the wolves of the sea, because they are such mighty hunters!

THE WANDERING ALBATROSS IS THE LARGEST SEABIRD IN THE WORLD, WITH A WINGSPAN OF UP TO 11 FEET! IT SPENDS MOST OF ITS TIME AT SEA IN THE SOUTHERN HEMISPHERE.

Cuddle Huddle

Emperor penguins huddle together in groups of up to 6,000 birds just to stay warm!

DID YOU KNOW?

The word "pinniped" means "wing-footed," and it is the name of the group of sea mammals made up of seals, sea lions, fur seals, and walruses.

Sea animals and seabirds feed on the fish and krill in the ocean.

Tropical Animals

WILD LOOKS

Orangutans have some pretty wild features—with arms 1½ times longer than their legs. And their bodies are not so small: The males are about 5 feet tall and 220 pounds. The females are about half as heavy. With age, the male orangutan develops large cheek and chest pouches that frame his face.

Mmm, Ants

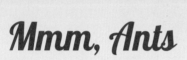

The anteater, a powerful digger, tunnels into anthills and termite mounds in search of food. It eats insects with the help of its long, sticky tongue, while its tough skin protects it from bug bites.

ACROBATIC

Orangutans are great acrobats. They prefer to travel by swinging rather than coming down from the trees and walking. In fact, orangutans are quite clumsy on the ground.

Weatherman

The jaguar is at home just about everywhere—mountains, grasslands, and rain forests. Everywhere it goes, the jaguar proclaims its presence with a mighty roar. Amazon Indians still believe that the roar of the jaguar is the sound of thunder that announces approaching rain.

TALK ABOUT IT

Apes and monkeys have many ways of warning each other of danger—and many ways of letting family or group members know what's on their minds. Howler monkeys are known for their howl, which sounds a little like a dog's bark and can be heard up to 2 miles away.

Marine Iguana

The marine iguana of the Galápagos islands, 600 miles off the coast of South America, is the only living lizard that has adapted to life in saltwater. It can dive as deep as 30 feet to find the seaweed it likes to eat.

Living the High Life

These animals all make themselves at home in the mountains of North America.

THE AGE OF A MOUNTAIN GOAT CAN BE DETERMINED BY COUNTING THE NUMBER OF RINGS ON ITS HORNS.

HEAVY-HEADED

The horns of a male bighorn sheep can weigh as much as the rest of its skeleton and curve almost into a circle.

Leaving Leftovers

Mountain lions hide their caught prey under leaves and soil so that they can come back to it for several days to eat.

WAY UP HIGH

The calliope hummingbird lives between 4,000 and 11,000 feet high in the mountains.

MOUNTAIN GOATS ARE NIMBLE CLIMBERS AND CAN JUMP NEARLY 12 FEET IN ONE LEAP.

Next Course, Please!

In order for an American pika to survive the winter, it must collect 50 times its bodyweight in food! When it cannot find enough of its regular food source, the pika eats its own poop.

Snow Shoes

The appropriately named snowshoe hare has large, furry feet that help it move on snow in winter. It changes coats for the colder season, turning from brown to white to blend in with its surroundings all year.

Spots and Stripes

At One with the Forest

The okapi has dark brown fur with white stripes on its upper legs and rump. When sunlight shines through the trees in the rain forests of central Africa, the okapi's stripes act as camouflage, helping it blend in with its surroundings and hide.

Giraffes are the **TALLEST** land animals on Earth.

THE OKAPI IS THE GIRAFFE'S ONLY KNOWN RELATIVE!

Hoofed Mammal Members

Hoofed mammals are divided into even-toed hoofed mammals and odd-toed hoofed mammals. Okapis and giraffes belong to the even-toed hoofed mammal group.

Privacy, Please!

Okapis are so shy that people in the western world didn't know they existed until Sir Harry Johnston's discovery in 1901.

When giraffes fight, they swing their long necks at their opponents to land blows that can be heard from over 325 feet away!

Giraffe Geography

Giraffes have different patterns of spots depending on where in Africa they live. Giraffes live in grasslands and open woodlands.

Word Search

Giraffe Family

Look at the puzzle below and see if you can find these words all about the giraffe family. Circle the words going across, up and down, and diagonally. Some words may be backwards!

AFRICA	RAIN FOREST
CAMOUFLAGE	SPOTS
EVEN-TOED	STRIPES
GRASSLAND	TALLEST
LONG NECK	WOODLAND

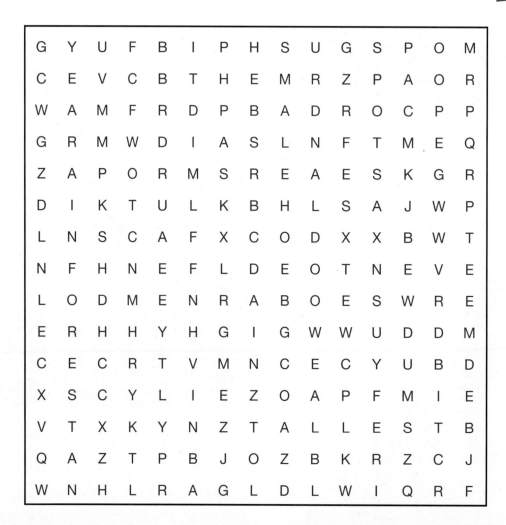

```
G Y U F B I P H S U G S P O M
C E V C B T H E M R Z P A O R
W A M F R D P B A D R O C P P
G R M W D I A S L N F T M E Q
Z A P O R M S R E A E S K G R
D I K T U L K B H L S A J W P
L N S C A F X C O D X X B W T
N F H N E F L D E O T N E V E
L O D M E N R A B O E S W R E
E R H H Y H G I G W W U D D M
C E C R T V M N C E C Y U B D
X S C Y L I E Z O A P F M I E
V T X K Y N Z T A L L E S T B
Q A Z T P B J O Z B K R Z C J
W N H L R A G L D L W I Q R F
```

Fun Facts about Hummingbirds

Listen carefully and you might hear the sound of the hummingbird. They are among the smartest birds in the world. Hummingbirds can remember every flower they've fed on and know how long it will take for the flower to refill its nectar.

Hummingbirds can fly backwards!

Hummingbirds do not suck nectar through their long bills. They lap it up with their tongues.

These birds have tiny hairs on the tips of their tongues that they use to lap up nectar.

Do you know how hummingbirds got their name? They flap their wings so fast that they make a humming sound.

Although they can't walk or hop on their feet, hummingbirds do use their feet to scoot sideways on branches.

Animal Habitats
Tundra

Tundra is a cold, dry, treeless region. Most of Earth's tundra is found in the Arctic.

DID YOU KNOW?

The Arctic tern flies between the Arctic and Antarctic, the longest route of any bird in the world! During the summer, this seabird lives and breeds in the Arctic region. Once winter falls, the tern flies halfway around the world to enjoy summer in the Antarctic.

CHILL OUT

The polar bear spends a lot of time traveling over Arctic sea ice on heavily furred, antislip paws. Its thick coat traps air and keeps the bear warm while it searches for food.

The snowy owl has feathers on its feet that act like slippers to keep it warm.

The polar bear has thick layers of fatty tissue, called blubber, that help it survive the freezing temperatures of the Arctic.

Fun Facts about Arctic Foxes

Arctic foxes live in the tundra. They can survive in some of the coldest temperatures in the Arctic—as low as 50 degrees below zero! How do these foxes survive such cold temperatures? They have one of the warmest coats of fur in the animal world. Their short ears, legs, and muzzle help them hold in heat so they don't get cold.

When Artic foxes hear an animal moving under the snow, they jump up and pounce on the snow to break through and get to their meal.

Depending on the season, there isn't always much food in the tundra for an Arctic fox to eat, so sometimes they eat a polar bear's leftovers.

Leafy Living

Swinging By

Gibbons are found in the rain forests of southern Asia. Their arms are much longer than their legs, allowing them to swing quickly from branch to branch.

Watch and Learn

Young bonobos learn what's safe to eat by watching the adults in the group.

DID YOU KNOW?

Chimpanzees are almost genetically identical to humans. Chimpanzees use sticks and stones as tools, similar to how humans use tools.

Apes, Great and Small

Gibbons are known as lesser apes, because they are much smaller than great apes such as chimpanzees and gorillas.

GRIN AND BEAR IT

Bonobos and chimpanzees are closely related. Bonobos have different grins for different emotions. They smile when they're stressed or scared, a smile known as a "fear grin," as well as when they're playing.

Singing Battle

Scary singing? Gibbons protect their territory from fellow gibbons by singing loudly in the early morning and late afternoon!

MOST ORANGUTANS AND ADULT HUMANS HAVE THE SAME NUMBER OF TEETH—32.

On Land and In Water

The tomato frog is native to Madagascar. To ward off predators, the frog will puff up its body to make itself look bigger. When it puffs up, its bright orange skin makes it look like a tomato!

Starting Out Wet

Young tiger salamanders have gills instead of lungs and can only breathe underwater. By adulthood, the salamanders have developed lungs and live on land.

The southern marbled newt makes its home near rivers, forests, and marshes in Spain and Portugal.

Masked Hopper

The wood frog is often recognized by the "mask," or coloring, around its eyes. Can you think of another animal that looks like it's wearing a mask?

AMPHIBIANS WERE THE FIRST TYPE OF VERTEBRATE TO WALK ON LAND. PICTURED HERE IS AN ERYOPS, A PREHISTORIC AMPHIBIAN.

Never Heard of 'Em!

Caecilians are the least-known amphibians. They have long, wormlike bodies with no limbs, and they live in tropical areas of the world.

Looks Like an Eel, Walks Like a...

The lesser siren has a long, slim body like an eel, and can be found in marshes, ponds, and other slow-moving bodies of water in the southern and central United States.

Common Creatures

Most newts and salamanders are found in wet, cool regions in the Northern Hemisphere, but there are a large number of species in Central and South America's tropical forests.

Wild at Heart

RABBIT EARS

The serval's big ears look more like they belong on a rabbit than a cat, but these ears serve the feline well. It can hear small animals hidden in the grass and then...pounce!

THE SAND CAT IS NOCTURNAL. IT SLEEPS DURING THE DAY AND HUNTS AT NIGHT FOR LIZARDS AND MICE.

Cat Couples

The jaguarundi looks more like a weasel than a cat. It has a long body, short legs, and a small head. Luckily, the male and female find each other attractive and, unlike most other cats, they live together for long periods of time.

Sleepyhead

Lions hunt, eat, and. . . sleep. Mostly sleep. It has been said that lions are the laziest animals in Africa. If they've had a good hunt and their bellies are full, lions can spend 16 to 20 hours a day resting or sleeping in the shade.

Slam Dunk

The caracal can leap into the air and swat a bird to the ground like a basketball player dunking a ball into the net. Its nickname is "desert lynx," because it lives in dry areas and its ear tufts are similar to those of the lynx.

Spotted Beauty

The ocelot has a coat of many colors. Its fur runs from reddish-brown to cream to white, with spots in a variety of shapes: solids, circles, and spots that join together to form stripes. The result is a masterpiece of camouflage and one of the most magnificent coats in the cat world.

Search & Find®
Monkey See, Monkey Do

Baboons are some of the largest types of monkeys and are considered the most dangerous. Like humans, baboons are social creatures, forming troops of anywhere from dozens to hundreds of baboons. These large groups can scare away trespassers. Male baboons use visual threats, like showing off their teeth, to ward off enemies.

**There are 6 baboons in the highlighted boxes.
Can you find each one hidden in the scene?**

Answers on page 224

Pig Family

Almost all domestic, or tame, pigs are descendants of the wild boar.

A Green Lifestyle

Wild pigs are found in forests and grasslands in Africa, Europe, and Asia.

WHAT A BOAR

A male pig is called a boar.

The warthog is a pig with a large head and long legs.

Built-in Bulldozer

There is a strong disk at the end of every pig's snout that works like the blade of a bulldozer, moving the soil when the pig hunts for food on the ground.

Nesting

Warthogs raise their young in burrows lined with grass.

Slow Movers

SLOWPOKES

Sloths are the slowest land mammals, creeping along at 0.15 miles per hour.

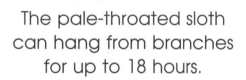

The pale-throated sloth can hang from branches for up to 18 hours.

SLOTHS ARE EXCELLENT SWIMMERS.

To Each Their Own

Some species of sloth have two toes on their front feet, and other species have three toes.

Night and Day

Two-toed sloths are nocturnal, while three-toed sloths are diurnal, or active during the day.

Good Host

A sloth's fur can be host to moths, beetles, cockroaches, and fungi.

DID YOU KNOW?

It can take a sloth up to a month to digest one meal.

Food Chain Scavengers

Animals that eat the remains of dead animals are called scavengers. Some examples of scavengers are vultures, hyenas, and opossums.

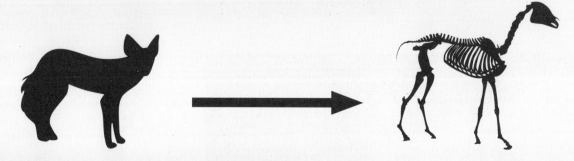

Carrion Dining

Scavengers, like these vultures, often swarm over carrion, which is the flesh of dead and rotting animals.

Reuse, Reduce, Recycle

While scavengers may eat gross food, they play an important role in the ecosystem, or community of animals living in the same habitat. They keep the ecosystem free of extra waste by recycling dead animals into the system as nutrients.

SUPER SEEKERS

Vultures are perfect for being scavengers; they have a strong sense of smell and excellent eyesight that helps them find their meals.

DID YOU KNOW?

Insects are often scavengers, but the blowfly doesn't eat dead animals. Instead, it lays its eggs in the open wounds of animals like cattle and sheep. Then the blowfly larvae, or maggots, eat the decaying flesh.

Substitute Scavengers

Other carnivores, like this coyote, will become scavengers if they see dead prey while hunting, but this is not their favorite meal.

FREE MEAL

Scavengers, like the opposum, are not picky eaters! They will eat the remains of animals that died through hunting, old age, or disease.

Waterfowl

Birds of a Feather

Mallards are thought to be the most abundant ducks on Earth. This means there are more of these kinds of ducks than any other.

Water World

Ducks and loons are known as waterfowl, birds generally found on or near the water.

COLD CLIMATE

The Baikal teal is a type of duck that lives and breeds in the cold Siberian forest. In the winter, it migrates to southeastern Asia.

Sizable Beauty

The mute swan is one of the heaviest flying birds in the world. It can weigh over 30 pounds!

DAD ON DUTY

The male African jacana sits on the eggs before they hatch and does most of the parenting for the chicks.

Hold Your Breath

Common loons can stay underwater for over 10 minutes.

Reptile Realm

BIG FAMILY

Skinks make up the largest family of lizards, with over 1,000 species in existence worldwide. The fire skink lives in the tropical forests of western Africa.

Here Be Dragon...Lizards

Dragon lizards are a group of reptiles including the frilled lizards and flying lizards. They are commonly found in Asia, Africa, and Australasia. All of these lizards have sharp teeth and feed mainly on insects, though larger species may eat small mammals and other lizards.

SOFT SHELLS

One group of freshwater turtles has lost most of the bone in the carapace, making their shells soft and leathery. They spend most of their time buried in mud or sand at the bottom of lakes and streams, waiting to catch unwary fish.

SKINK HIJINKS

Skinks are teeny lizards that live near tree stumps or decaying driftwood. The male five-lined skink chooses a mate by nipping at the necks of other skinks. If a skink bites back, it's a male; but if it stays still or runs off, it's a female!

Legless Lizard

Have you ever heard of a scheltopusik? This apparently legless lizard, also known as a European glass lizard or giant glass lizard, can easily be confused with a snake. The best way to tell a scheltopusik apart from a snake is by its eyelids and ear openings, neither of which are present in snakes. In reality, the scheltopusik has two tiny rear leg stubs near the base of its tail!

Fashionable Frills

The frilled lizard lives in the trees of Australia's tropical woodlands. It is the only reptile to have a large "collar" of skin around its neck, called a frill. Male frilled lizards fan out their frills to scare away predators and before fighting each other during breeding season.

Cats Hot and Cool

Tuned In

A cat with antennae? The lynx has long, glossy, black tufts that stick up from each ear. Like hearing aids, they increase the cat's ability to detect the slightest sound. No creak, snap, or thump in the snowbound woods gets by the listening lynx.

Cat for All Climates

Cougars, also known as pumas, panthers, or mountain lions, can be found on cold, high peaks, in steaming jungles, in swamplands, and even in deserts.

A Cat Called Bob

The bobcat is named for its stubby 6-inch tail, which appears to be "bobbed," or cut short. The bobcat weighs about 20 pounds and looks very much like its cousin the lynx. The bobcat prowls most of North America.

Phantom of the Forest

Bobcats have favorite places—ledges, tree limbs, and trails—that they come back to again and again. Finding one of these sites may be the only way to lay eyes on a bobcat. These quick-as-a-wink cats are usually seen as fast flashes of fur in the forest.

Disappearing Spots

Adult cougars have sleek, tawny coats that match their spooky yellow eyes, but cougar cubs are spotted with black. At six months, the cubs begin to lose their spots and become cats of one color.

KILLER COUGAR

A large male cougar is 200 pounds of muscle. A fierce predator, he can kill a deer with one powerful bite. In his territory, no other animal can challenge him—except a barking dog. The yapping of a poodle sends a cougar up a tree.

Got Your Goat

Crowning Glory

The markhor is the largest wild goat, found in the mountains of Central Asia. Markhors are easily recognizable by their magnificent spiral horns, which can grow to around 5 feet in males. Female markhor horns only grow up to 10 inches.

CHANGE OF CLOTHES

The takin is an even-toed hoofed mammal that is often referred to as a goat-antelope, though it is most closely related to sheep. Takins grow a thicker, secondary layer of fur in the winter months and shed it in the summer—just like a winter coat!

Hidden Treasure

The Sichuan takin is a type of takin that lives in the Himalayan mountains in China and bordering regions. It is considered a national treasure in China.

HOT TOPIC

The Nubian ibex is the only species of ibex that lives in hot, dry regions. A shiny coat of short fur keeps the ibex cool by reflecting the sunlight.

Word Search

Endangered Mammals

Look at the puzzle below and see if you can find the names of these endangered animals. Circle the words going across, up and down, and diagonally. Some words may be backwards!

ADDAX	GORILLA
BENGAL TIGER	MARKHOR
BLACK RHINO	ORANGUTAN
BONOBO	PANGOLIN
GIBBON	RED PANDA

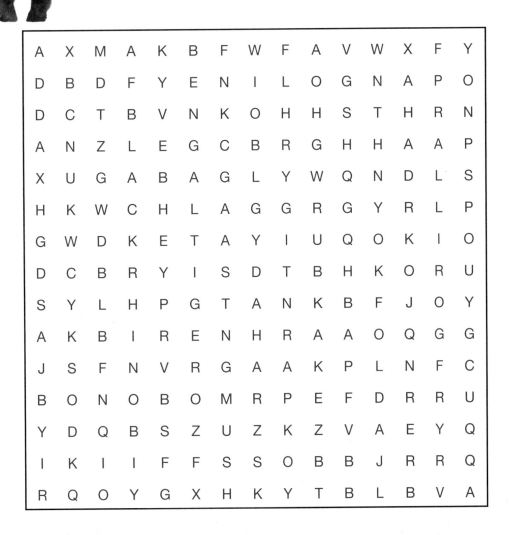

```
A X M A K B F W F A V W X F Y
D B D F Y E N I L O G N A P O
D C T B V N K O H H S T H R N
A N Z L E G C B R G H H A A P
X U G A B A G L Y W Q N D L S
H K W C H L A G G R G Y R L P
G W D K E T A Y I U Q O K I O
D C B R Y I S D T B H K O R U
S Y L H P G T A N K B F J O Y
A K B I R E N H R A A O Q G G
J S F N V R G A A K P L N F C
B O N O B O M R P E F D R R U
Y D Q B S Z U Z K Z V A E Y Q
I K I I F F S S O B B J R R Q
R Q O Y G X H K Y T B L B V A
```

Antelopes

HERD MENTALITY

The addax is a critically endangered antelope that lives in the Sahara desert. It is one of the few species in which females and males have horns of the same size. Addaxes are not very fast runners, so living in herds helps to provide protection from predators.

ON THE RISE

The klipspringer is a dwarf antelope living in rocky outcrops and cliffs in central and eastern Africa. It's only about 20 inches tall!

Jump for Joy...or Fear

When the springbok is scared or excited, it will bounce up and down on stiff legs–just like its relative the gazelle. This movement is called pronking, and it can lift the springbok several feet in the air.

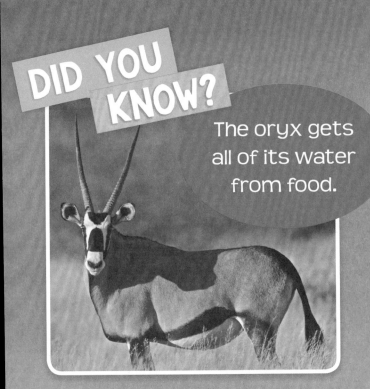

The oryx gets all of its water from food.

COMEBACK KID

The scimitar-horned oryx is a North African antelope that became extinct in the wild by the end of the 1900s because of over-hunting, drought, and loss of food. Some wildlife centers have started to reintroduce them to the wild.

Welcome Back

The Souss Massa National Park is a site used in part for the reintroduction of antelopes such as the addax antelope, dorcas gazelle (below), and scimitar-horned oryx.

Antelopes, like most even-toed hoofed mammals, are herbivores.

Snakes on the Move

Serpentine Slither

Some snakes seem to dart from side to side, moving forward in a series of "S" curves.

In actuality, the snake is using its ribs and pushing off against anything it can get a grip on.

THE BIG SQUEEZE

Pythons, boas, and their relatives really know how to squeeze the life out of prey. These constrictors grasp prey in their mouths and coil around it. They constrict, or squeeze, the prey until it can no longer breathe.

HEAVYWEIGHT

The green anaconda is the largest boa and the heaviest snake in the world.

SIDEWINDING

Sidewinding is the special form of locomotion developed by desert snakes, because it's hard to grip the soft, shifting sand. The sidewinder rattlesnake moves from left to right, leaving a "J"-shaped track in the sand.

WHAT A HOG

The western hognose snake lives in prairies, meadows, and plains, in the Central United States, southern Canada, and northern Mexico. This snake gets its name from its upturned, hoglike nose.

Concertina Movement

A snake climbs a tree with the motion of a concertina, which is a small accordion. Gripping the bark with abdominal plates, the snake sends its head moving up the tree.

Songbirds

A Song in Their Hearts

Songbirds make up over half of the bird species in the world. They belong to a group of perching birds called passerines.

Precious Cargo

American robins lay beautiful pale blue eggs, which is where we get the color robin's-egg blue! Females generally lay between three and seven eggs at a time.

GREAT ESCAPE

The red-whiskered bulbul is native to Asia and has been introduced in the United States, Australia, New Zealand, and islands in the Pacific and Indian Oceans. It was first introduced in the United States when some birds escaped from an aviary in Miami!

Air Acrobat

The raven is known for its acrobatic flight, twisting and turning at high speeds. Ravens can even roll over and fly upside down!

HOUSE HUNTERS

House martins almost always build their mud nests on buildings, under roofs on houses and barns.

Winter Traveler

The snow bunting lives in the Arctic tundra in the summer and moves to mountainsides and coastal areas in the winter. It has a short, cone-shaped beak that helps it peel seeds.

Big Birds

Flightless Wonders

Emus are the largest birds in Australia and the second largest birds in the world, right behind the ostrich. An emu may travel hundreds of miles to find food and water!

OSTRICHES HAVE THE LARGEST EYES OF ANY LAND ANIMAL.

STEERING WINGS

The greater rhea has surprisingly long wings for a bird that can't fly! Its wings work like an airplane rudder to help the rhea dodge predators. The rhea also uses its wings for balance while running.

Doting Dads

In most large flightless birds, the male incubates, or sits on, the eggs until they hatch. He also takes care of the chicks alone.

DID YOU KNOW?

People in South America use rhea feathers to make feather dusters!

Swift Kick

The southern cassowary has dagger-like claws and an extremely powerful kick, making it one of the world's most dangerous birds.

OSTRICHES CAN SPRINT OVER 40 MILES PER HOUR.

Weasel Family

TIGHT SQUEEZE

The least weasel has such a slim body, it can squeeze through a hole the size of an adult human finger!

Half and Half

Ferrets are so closely related to polecats that the two species can breed to produce polecat-ferret hybrids, a cross between the two animals.

SWIM FANS

Minks spend a lot of time swimming, so they have an extra-thick coat to protect them from the cold water. In the past, American minks were trapped by the thousands for their fur.

All black-footed ferrets alive today are descended from just 18 animals! This species was thought to be extinct until a small population was discovered in 1981. Eighteen ferrets were caught and kept by conservation centers to breed before being reintroduced into the wild.

SIGNATURE SCENT

All members of the weasel family have a gland or small sac near their bottoms that releases a strong-smelling scent. While skunks use this scent as self-defense, polecats use the smell to mark their territory.

TOTAL TRANSFORMATION

The tip of a stoat's tail is always black, but the rest of its fur changes color for winter. The stoat is reddish-brown in summer, and it turns white in winter to blend in with the snow. When the stoat is wearing its winter coat, it is known as an ermine.

Big Leap

Martens are the best climbers of the weasel family. They can leap between tree branches like cats!

Up All Night

These creatures are all nocturnal.

FEELING THE HEAT

The eyelash viper has heat-sensitive pits on its head between the nostrils and eyes that it uses to detect the heat of warm-blooded animals.

ALL BALLED UP

A slow loris sleeps during the day in a very specific position. It curls into a ball with its head between its legs.

No Appetite

The luna moth only lives for about a week after leaving its cocoon, and it won't eat during that time.

The Indian flying fox learns to fly when it is 11 weeks old.

Loud and Clear

Sugar gliders are very vocal: They scream, hiss, and produce a high-pitched bark!

DIZZYING DISPLAY

Red-eyed tree frogs use their brightly colored legs and eyes to confuse their predators so they have a chance to escape.

Elephants

Sensitive Side

An elephant's skin is very sensitive, so it must bathe often to cool off and help keep the insects away.

AFRICAN ELEPHANTS FLAP THEIR LARGE EARS CONSTANTLY IN ORDER TO KEEP THEIR BODIES COOL.

Family First

There may only be around 30,000 Asiatic elephants left in the world, living in the tropical forests of Asia. These elephants are herbivores, and they live in small family units led by the oldest female.

Asian elephants weigh nearly 11,000 pounds—that's about the same weight as four cars!

Elephants use their trunks like straws! They suck up water and then release it in their mouths.

Drink Up

Asian elephants never stray far from a source of fresh water because they need to drink at least once a day.

The African elephant is the largest living land mammal, weighing as much as 8 tons.

Marsupial Mates

WARNING SIGNS

Wallaroos will thump their feet to warn others of danger, and they will make hissing sounds if they feel threatened.

On the Island

The pademelon is extinct on mainland Australia, but these marsupials are abundant in Tasmania.

LEAPS AND BOUNDS

The yellow-footed rock wallaby lives on mountaintops and can leap up to 13 feet high in the air.

Opossums can have up to 25 babies at once!

Digging for Dinner

The long-nosed potoroo's diet is mostly made up of underground fungi that it digs up with its strong front paws.

Different Folks

Numbats are marsupials, but they don't have pouches for their young. Instead, they have folds of skin and long hair on their chests that protect their babies.

Safer Down Under

Wombats are rarely seen in the wild, because they are nocturnal and spend their days in underground burrows that protect them from the heat and from predators.

Primates Aplenty

WHAT'S A LEMUR?

The lemur is a prosimian, a relative of apes and monkeys, found only on the island of Madagascar. With its whiskers and large ears, the ring-tailed lemur looks more like a cat than a monkey.

Listen Up!

Bush babies may be tiny primates, but they are surprisingly noisy, making clucking and croaking sounds, cries, and shrill whistles. The cry of a bush baby sounds just like a human infant!

The Special One

The tarsier is in a group by itself. To primatologists, the people who study primates, this creature has a strange mix of traits. It has the large eyes and ears of the prosimians, but has a short nose like monkeys and apes.

Planting Seeds

Red-ruffed lemurs help to pollinate rain forest plants. When these lemurs drink flower nectar, pollen sticks to their fur. Pollen from a lemur's fur will rub off on other flowers as it travels, allowing the plants to reproduce.

JUMP ON IT

Sifakas are a type of lemur that move by jumping sideways on their hind legs, holding their arms out for balance. When they move through the air at great speeds, they look like they're dancing!

Ghostly Gaze

The word "lemur" comes from the Latin *lemures*, meaning "ghost." The Malagasy people associated lemurs with spirits, because lemurs are nocturnal and have large eyes and an eerie stare.

Male ringtail lemurs have scent glands on their wrists and forearms. They use them for "stink fights" with other males, wiping their tails across those glands and then waving their tails at each other. This is how they compete for female attention.

Small Measure

Mouse lemurs are some of the smallest primates of all. They can be as small as 2½ inches!

Macaques

Snow Monkey

The Japanese macaque has adapted to a harsh environment, enduring snowy winters in the mountains on rugged Honshu Island. Once the trees have shed their leaves, the macaque gets through the cold season by feeding on bark.

I'M BLUSHING

During breeding season, the macaques' expressive and unique red faces become brighter.

Barbary Variety

The Barbary macaque is the only macaque species living outside of Asia. Barbary macaques are native to Morocco and Algeria, and a small population was introduced on Gibraltar.

No Tail to Tell

Barbary macaques are also known as Barbary apes because they have no tail

Word Search
Primates

Look at the puzzle below and see if you can find the names of these primates. Circle the words going across, up and down, and diagonally. Some words may be backwards!

APE	HUMAN
BABOON	LEMUR
BUSH BABY	MACAQUE
CAPUCHIN	MONKEY
CHIMPANZEE	TARSIER

```
K G D N Y O B P M I V B E H J
I U O E L K G A Z T L E P S E
T C J I I N C C G J Z N B L N
A Y A N B A G R G N A P E L Z
R R I P Q B J I A U O I Q P H
S U X U U V A P P J I V L Q N
I M E Q S C M B U S H B A B Y
E E S D A I H L U I R V W S S
R L D Y H T C I U V U H V M T
N A B C P H V J N M U G N Z I
P O W B C X Q B G M H V F N A
P B O R W L M Y A T A D V B V
P C I B C F M N H B V L J Y F
P G N U A A R H Y E K N O M O
V D I L E B D Q Y X U M J V L
```

Taking Flight

THE BALD EAGLE IS THE NATIONAL BIRD OF THE UNITED STATES.

FISH ON THE MENU

Ninety-nine percent of the osprey's meals are made up of fish, so ospreys need to live near ponds, rivers, lakes, and coasts.

TIGHT GRIP

Bald eagles have a grip that is 10 times stronger than a human's.

Moody Dresser

High-speed Hunters

Golden eagles can dive at their prey at speeds of 150 miles per hour.

THRILL OF THE CHASE

Goshawks can be very persistent. They are known to chase snowshoe hares for 45 to 60 minutes until the goshawks can corner the hares and scoop them up.

The ornate hawk eagle has a crest of feathers on its head that can be raised or lowered depending on its mood. A raised crest means that the bird is excited or curious.

Meal Prep

Harpy eagles don't have to hunt every day. If they catch large prey, they can stash them in a tree to save for the next day.

New Zealand Natives

A RARE SIGHT

The New Zealand sea lion is one of the rarest sea lions in the world due to overhunting and a limited breeding range.

Helping Gardens Grow

Tuis are endemic, or native, birds of New Zealand. They are important pollinators for the country's plants.

THE KIWI HAS A LONG BEAK THAT IT CAN PUSH ALL THE WAY INTO THE GROUND TO SEARCH FOR FOOD.

The Tuatara

The tuatara is the last living member of an ancient group of reptiles. When dinosaurs roamed the Earth, the tuatara's relatives were spread around the world. Today, tuataras live on just a few islands near New Zealand. The Maori people of New Zealand named it for its distinctive crest: "Tuatara" means "spiny back."

Slow Start

Tuatara eggs take take from 12 to 15 months to hatch, and babies take from 9 to 14 years to mature— longer than any other reptile. A tuatara's life is long, though, lasting up to 100 years.

THE WETA

Weta are unique-looking insects that have big bodies, spiny legs, and curved tusks.

Suits of Armor

These scaly mammals look alike and are sometimes confused for one another, but they are actually not related!

HARD BODY

An armadillo is a small mammal covered with hard, bony plates with skin in between that lets the creature twist and curl. The nine-banded armadillo lives in the southeastern United States, rooting for insects or vegetables, and eating with its pointy, sticky tongue.

SCALY

Sometimes described as a "walking pinecone," the giant pangolin of Africa is covered with thick, overlapping scales. The pangolin uses its strong front claws to tear into termite mounds and ant nests. It slurps up the insects with a tongue that may be as long as 28 inches.

Pangolins are also called scaly anteaters because of their favorite food.

STOP, DROP, AND ROLL

The hard plates covering an armadillo's body are called scutes. When frightened, a three-banded armadillo may dig into the ground, crouch, or roll into a ball, leaving only its scutes exposed and giving a predator very little to bite. The three-banded armadillo is the only species that can envelop itself in its scutes.

Get Rolling

Unlike armadillos, all species of pangolins can roll themselves into balls to defend themselves from predators.

The nine-banded armadillo almost always gives birth to identical quadruplets.

Dingoes and Jackals

Dingoes and jackals are members of the dog family.

UNWELCOME GUESTS

The dingo preys on small animals, such as rodents, rabbits, lizards, and birds, but it also eats sheep. Farmers may kill dingoes to protect their farm animals.

FITTING IN

The dingo is able to blend in with its desertlike habitat because of its sandy or reddish coat.

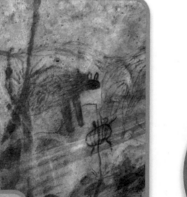

Top Dogs

Dingoes were introduced in Australia between 3,000 and 4,000 years ago. They are now the main predator on the continent. Australian aboriginals, or natives, even included dingoes in rock paintings like this one.

Fenced Out

A dingo fence was built in the 1800s to protect grazing lands for Australia's sheep.

212

Wild Dogs

All three species of jackals live in Africa. The species differ mainly in appearance and in habitat. Golden jackals also live in parts of Europe and Asia. They can be found in deserts, arid grasslands, and savannas. The golden jackal has sandy-colored fur.

DIFFERENT STRIPES

The side-striped jackal is found in marshes, bushlands, savannas, and mountains. This jackal has a duller coat than the other species, with a white tip on its tail and stripes on the sides of its body.

SILVER STREAK

Black-backed jackals, also known as silver-backed jackals, live mainly in woodlands and savannas. The black-backed jackal has red or reddish-brown fur with a black or silver back.

Earth Pigs

Aardvarks get their name from the South African language of Afrikaans. *Aardvark* means "earth pig."

NO CLEAR VISION

Aardvarks are color-blind and have poor vision, so they rely on their senses of sound and smell to help them find food and avoid predators.

FAMILY TREE

Even though aardvarks look like pigs, they are more closely related to elephants and golden moles.

EAGER TO EAT

When aardvarks are hunting for food, they can dig holes 2 feet deep in just 15 seconds.

Take Cover

When an aardvark feels threatened, it can dig a hole and cover itself with dirt in about 10 minutes.

NIGHT OWLS

Aardvarks are mostly active at night and spend the day curled up in a ball, sleeping in burrows.

THE AARDVARK'S TONGUE IS 12 INCHES LONG AND IS STICKY TO HELP IT CATCH INSECTS TO EAT.

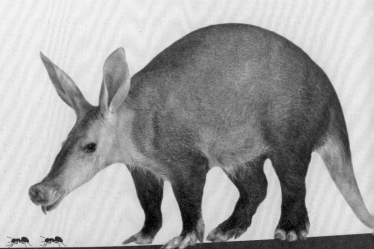

Tigers

Mystery, courage, fierceness—these are the characteristics of the biggest wild cat of them all, the tiger.

Shadowy Figures

The tiger's magnificent orange-and-black striped coat is not just for decoration. Stripes are the perfect camouflage in tall grasses and forests, where strips of light filter to the ground through dense leaves. Tigers that live in the northern climates are lighter in color to help them hide in the snow.

BEATING THE HEAT

It's hot in the jungle—steamy and sticky. Among big cats, the tiger may be the most likely to cool off in the water. Splashing, swimming, lounging up to its neck in lakes and rivers, the tiger knows how to get relief from the heat.

Pale Face

A white tiger is not a ghost. It is a Bengal tiger that gets its coloring from a rare gene. The white tiger has a pink nose and charcoal- or chocolate-colored stripes on a white background, and its eyes may be blue—a tiger of a different hue!

The Stealth Attack

Rarely seen, the tiger hunts alone at night. It creeps up under cover and gets as close as possible to its prey. Then it takes a great leap at the victim and strikes with a lethal weapon—the largest canine teeth of any meat-eating land animal. Still, hunting is not easy. Tigers catch only about one out of every 20 animals they go after.

Tiger Tots

Tiger cubs are born into a world that can be very hard. They may be killed by other animals while their mother is hunting. At 18 months to two years old, they leave their mother to find their own territories.

FIVE TYPES OF TIGERS ROAM VARIOUS PARTS OF ASIA. THE LARGEST IS THE SIBERIAN TIGER, WHICH CAN BE MORE THAN 10 FEET LONG AND WEIGH OVER 600 POUNDS.

Mighty Monotremes

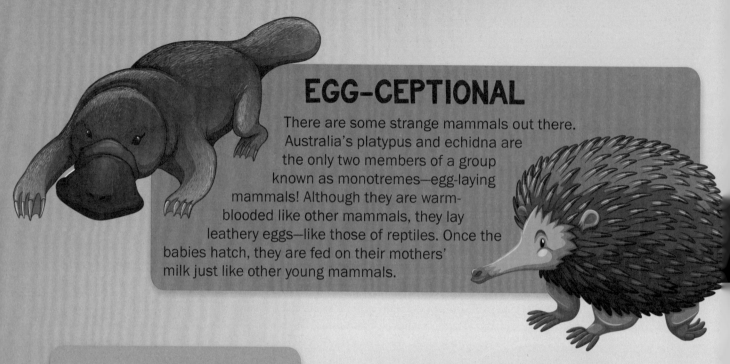

EGG-CEPTIONAL

There are some strange mammals out there. Australia's platypus and echidna are the only two members of a group known as monotremes—egg-laying mammals! Although they are warm-blooded like other mammals, they lay leathery eggs—like those of reptiles. Once the babies hatch, they are fed on their mothers' milk just like other young mammals.

EARLY RELATIONS

Scientists believe that monotremes may be the earliest relatives of modern mammals.

ECHIDNAS ROLL UP INTO A BALL, WITH ONLY THEIR SPIKY SPINES VISIBLE, IN ORDER TO PROTECT THEMSELVES. ECHIDNAS HAVE ONLY ONE NATURAL ENEMY—HUMANS!

MALE PLATYPUSES HAVE SPURS ON THEIR PAWS THAT RELEASE TOXIC VENOM.

DAILY GRIND

Platypuses and echidnas have no teeth. Instead, they grind food with the bony plates in their mouths. Long snouts that look like bills or beaks help these egg-laying mammals detect prey.

The platypus is an excellent swimmer.

F-ants-y That!

The echidna is also called a spiny anteater because of its spiny body and its taste for ants.

BOTTOM FEEDER

The duck-billed platypus is a bottom feeder, diving down to feed on shellfish, insects, and worms. Like other platypuses, the duck-billed platypus uses its bill to stir up the river bottom for its meals. The bits of gravel and earth it picks up with its snout when it goes in to eat help to break down its food.

Fun Facts about Animal Names

Peregrine falcons get their name from the Latin *peregrinus*, meaning "pilgrim" or "wanderer."

In Malaysia, the word "orangutan" means "person of the forest."

Jaguars get their name from the Native American word *yaguar*, meaning "he who kills with one leap."

"Rhinoceros" means "nose horn."

Hippopotamus means "river horse" in Greek.

Helping Hands

These organizations work to save animals.

The **International Fund for Animal Welfare** wants to save animals and their habitats. The group has more than 40 projects, including protecting seals, whales, elephants, and tigers. They also rescue pets.

The **Wildlife Conservation Society** works to conserve the habitats of wild animals. Workers at this organization are concerned about climate change, extinction, human-wildlife coexistence, and sustainability.

PAWS is all about people helping animals. This group helps rehabilitate injured and orphaned wildlife, shelters and adopts homeless pets, and educates people to help make the world a better place for animals.

The **World Wildlife Fund** (WWF) is an organization that works to protect the environment and animals through science, and with help from local and global groups.

The **African Wildlife Foundation** works in Africa to protect ecosystems and wildlife, and to create a more peaceful relationship between humans and wildlife.

Gorilla Doctors is a team of veterinarians in Rwanda, Uganda, and the National Republic of the Congo that helps treat diseases and rescue wounded mountain gorillas to save them from extinction.

Answers

Page 10

Word Scramble
Amazing Animal Jobs

Unscramble the letters to spell the names of animal jobs.
Which job sounds the most exciting to you?
Write it down in the space at the bottom of the page!

LSTOGOIOZ
Z O O L O G I S T

MANALI RENTIAR
A N I M A L   T R A I N E R

EPT ROERGOM
P E T   G R O O M E R

LAMINA TORLCON RECFOIF
A N I M A L   C O N T R O L
O F F I C E R

NAVEINATIRER
V E T E R I N A R I A N

NALIMA SITRATHPE
A N I M A L   T H E R A P I S T

_____

Page 35

Penguin Maze
Home Sweet Home

Ever get lost? Imagine looking for your parents among millions of others! Luckily, in the penguin world, chicks and parents recognize each other's calls and always find one another. A chick calls out even as it breaks out of its egg so the parent will get to know its voice.

This baby penguin wandered away from the rookery and got lost! Follow the maze to help the baby penguin find his mom.

START

FINISH

Page 49

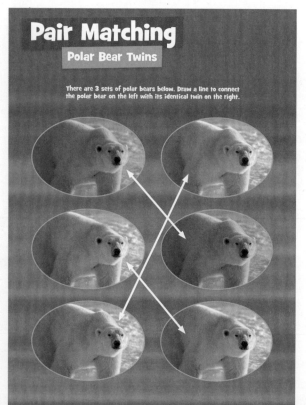

Pair Matching
Polar Bear Twins

There are 3 sets of polar bears below. Draw a line to connect the polar bear on the left with its identical twin on the right.

Pages 88-89

Search & Find®
Prickly Situation

The porcupine may be slow and a little clumsy, but it has a unique way of protecting itself from predators. Once startled, a porcupine will prepare for attack by bristling up its 30,000 sharp spines, or quills, and stabbing the enemy with its dangerous points. The quills are released and embedded in the attacker, and the porcupine will regrow quills to replace lost ones.

There are 6 porcupines in the highlighted boxes. Can you find each one hidden among the other forest animals?

Answers

Page 107

Fill in the Blanks
Fascinating Animal Facts

Fill in the missing letters to complete the fun animal facts below. Then write the numbered letters in order at the bottom of the page to find out which animal no longer lives in the wild!

The smallest bird in the world is the
H U M M I N G B I R D.
‾1‾

The only relative of the giraffe is the
O K A P I.
‾2‾

An animal that is active at night and sleeps during the day is
N O C T U R N A L.
‾3‾

This animal is often known as man's best friend:
D O G.
‾4‾

Ducks have no nerves in their
F E E T.
‾5‾

Animals that have no backbone are called
I N V E R T E B R A T E S.
‾6‾

This animal makes its own natural sunscreen:
H I P P O P O T A M U S.
‾7‾

Puffins have waterproof
F E A T H E R S.
‾8‾

Answer: The G O L D F I S H
1 2 3 4 5 6 7 8

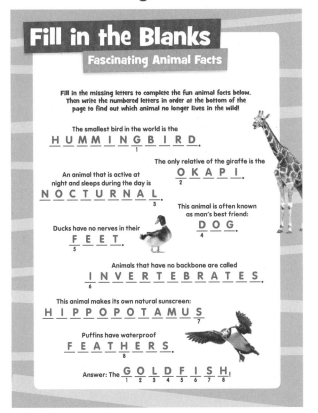

Page 117

Spot the Difference
Busy Bee

Find and circle 10 differences between these two pictures.

Page 127

Jungle Maze
Going Bananas

Time for a snack! Follow the maze to help the monkey reach the bananas.

FINISH

START

Page 139

Secret Science Code
The Name Game

To help scientists identify animals, they give each animal a two-part Latin name. The first word in its name is the genus that animal belongs to, and the second word represents its species.

Use the key below to crack the code and find out the Latin names of these gazelles!

A = 1 C = 2 D = 3 E = 4 G = 5 H = 6 I = 7
M = 8 N = 9 O = 10 R = 11 S = 12 T = 13 U = 14

The dama gazelle is known to scientists as
N A N G E R D A M A
9 1 9 5 4 11 3 1 8 1

Thomson's gazelle is called
E U D O R C A S
4 14 3 10 11 2 1 12
T H O M S O N I I
13 6 10 8 12 10 9 7 7

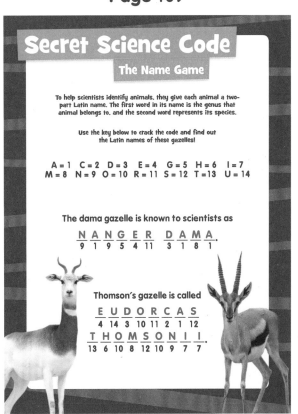

Answers

Page 160

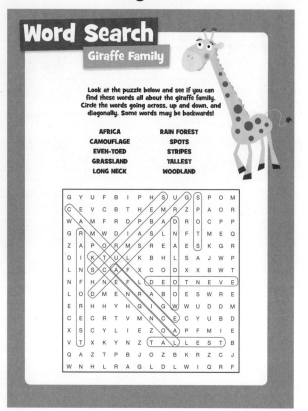

Pages 170-171

Page 185

Page 205

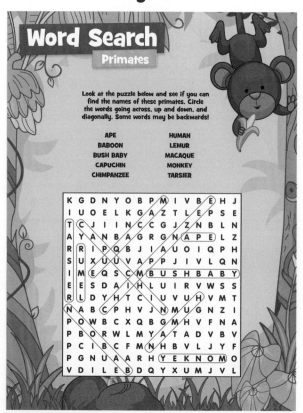